COUNTED CORPSE

STITCHES IN CRIME - BOOK 4

ACF BOOKENS

1

———

I tucked my crowbar under the wood and began the dance of prying it off without breaking it. As I worked, I let my mind play back through my memories.

I practically grew up in the manse, the pastor's house, at the church my parents' attended when I was a kid. The pastor's daughter, Sue Ellen, was my best friend, and since my mom was the church music director and the manse was next door, I was there on the church grounds most days.

Sue Ellen was a bit more of a girly girl than I was, or at least her mama thought her one, so she had all these creepy, pristine porcelain dolls that sat on high shelves in her third-floor bedroom. Their frilly dresses and lace caps always puzzled me because it made no sense to me to have toys that you couldn't play with, but Sue Ellen knew better. She knew that some of her role as the pastor's kid was to be a show piece, just like those dolls. That's why she stifled most of her screams when her mother dragged a stiff brush through her, curly, coarse blonde hair on Sunday mornings so that it would look perfect in braids.

I never had that pressure to look perfect, maybe *act* perfect, but never look, and today, as I tightened the bandana over my hair and prepared to pull down the crown molding in this other pastor's house near Bethel Church, I was grateful. My job as an architectural salvager didn't leave much space for primping.

This job had been a long time coming. The deacons at the church had asked me to come in and salvage some key pieces that they wanted to put into their new church addition, and if I would, they were happy to give me anything else I wanted from the hundred-year-old house. They wanted the simple chandelier from the front foyer, the mantel from the parlor, and a lovely old door that led to the dirt-floored basement. Everything else was mine, and I was determined to make the most of this gift.

I'd already hauled out the door and chandelier, and I was just waiting for help from my friend Saul's crew to get out the heavy wooden mantel. Meanwhile, I was doing what I could on my own and popping off as much of the simple but lovely woodwork as I could without damaging it. This molding and the baseboards would be lovely in a farmhouse, and what wasn't salvageable for architecture, Dad would use to make vintage picture frames that I could sell at my soon-to-open salvage store, Paisley's Architectural Salvage.

Architectural salvage had been my career since I had my son and my marriage fell apart more than a year ago. It was flexible in hours, made use of my background in history, and let me feed my desire to go into old buildings without putting me in danger of breaking the law.

This latest job was special because I was, as of two weeks ago, the only white member of Bethel Church, a historically black congregation, and I was eager to do a good job for my new church family, especially after they'd welcomed me so full-heartedly into their pews and hearts.

"Do you want me to try to get this wainscotting down?" My friend and fellow Bethel member Mary Johnson shouted from around the corner in the dining room. "It's pretty, but do you need it?"

I walked through the cased doorway from the study to the dining room and could almost imagine the large, farm table where the pastor and his family had Sunday lunches with different church members after services each week. Mary was poised with her crowbar ready to pull off the dark walnut veneer, and I smiled at her commitment.

Mary and I had become friends when an earlier salvage job had brought me into her life because of her history with an old store in our county, and since then, we'd just grown closer and closer. Now, since she loved this old house and had spent a lot of time here as a child, I'd asked if I could hire her for the day to help me salvage. She had refused payment, but I had a scheme involving an old Singer sewing machine I'd found a couple jobs back and some vintage quilts I'd bought at a flea market. The gift was waiting on her porch, thanks to the generosity of my dad and step-mom, Lucille, for her to find when she got home.

"Yeah, let's see if we can get the pieces off whole," I said as I joined Mary with my own prybar. "If we can, they'll sell for a pretty penny, or maybe the church would even want them for the new fellowship hall?"

"Now that's an idea," Mary said. "We're already putting the mantel in there, so this would make for that cool, old-study feel, wouldn't it?"

I smiled and gently slipped my bar beneath the chair rail at the top as Mary did the same. She was really a natural at this work, and before long, we had gotten all the rails and baseboards off and were well on our way to salvaging more than half of the wainscotting. It looked like the church would have beautiful walnut walls if they wanted them.

As we were about to tug off the last sheet, Saul called from the front door, "Muscle men reporting for duty."

I laughed at my best friend Mika's uncle and put down my tools to meet him. He was alone in the door, and I said, "Are you the muscle because no offense—"

"Stop right there, young lady. I'll have you know I can still pick you up and throw you over my shoulder like a sack of potatoes if you don't mind yourself." He smiled.

"Right, respect my elders. Got it." I laughed as Saul glared at me. "Thanks for coming. The mantel is this way."

I led him through another cased doorway into the small parlor that sat opposite the study, and he whistled. "What a beauty," he said as he ran his fingers over the fine oak grain in the delicately carved wood. "They went all out on this one."

Mary joined us and said, "They did, but the members did all the work. The church records show that the tree from which this mantel was made was felled from a member's land, and one of the congregation's founding members had become a master carpenter when he was a slave. So he did the carving."

I took a deep breath. "I didn't know that. Wow." I joined Saul in caressing the wood. "Let's take extra care, okay?"

Saul nodded. "If it's alright, I'd like to have the piece professionally cleaned for the church, nothing that will change the finish or take off much of the patina. Just shine it up for the new addition. Would that be alright?"

Mary laughed. Saul was always doing very generous things like this, and we had all learned to give him the joy of accepting them without fuss. "Of course, Saul. Thank you. I'll let the deacon board know."

Two young, muscular men walked in, and I said, "Ah, finally, some muscles."

Saul scowled at me and then smiled. "Gentlemen, take care with this beauty. Paisley, you already detached it?"

"All but this one place. I didn't want it falling over. Just a sec." I slipped my smallest pry bar behind the mantel and gently wiggled the final nail from the plaster. As the mantel began to tip forward, the two men took hold of it and lifted it between them with, it seemed, no strain. The piece must have weighed four-hundred pounds, but the two of them carried it out with less effort than it took me to wield a fifty-pound bag of chicken feed from the farm co-op.

With the mantel loaded and off with the chandelier and door to a professional architectural restorer – Saul insisted on having everything cleaned – Mary and I finished up the wainscotting, loaded the used moving truck that I had bought at auction for hauling my goods, and decided to do a final walkthrough of the house.

I'd carefully scoured every room on my past visits, but I had, for reasons involving spiders and damp and too many scary movies, avoided the basement. Mary had assured me there wasn't much down there, but I still felt like I needed to take a look, just to be sure. Now that Mary was with me, it seemed kind of silly that I hadn't done it before, especially since the demolition crew was set to come and clear the ground in three days. Nothing like waiting until the last minute to scour a full thousand square feet of space.

Mary and I went down the creaky wooden staircase and stepped into a slightly musty but otherwise completely pleasant basement. The dirt floor was hard-packed and felt like concrete, and the spiders were really minimal. Mary was right, though, the space was mostly empty. There were a few old wooden shelves that had probably once held jars full of pickles and canned tomatoes, and I made a note to carry those out and clean them up since they'd look great in Mika's yarn shop.

I felt the twinge of heartbreak when Mary cracked open the rounded top of an old steamer truck and watched it crumble to dust in her hand. The trunk was empty, though, so while it was sad to not have the vessel itself, it didn't hold any secret treasures like rare carnival glass or something.

Otherwise, the space was empty, and I felt a pang of sadness that we hadn't discovered a trove of old family treasures stored below ground. It was just as well though because the damp would, as the trunk revealed, destroy most everything.

We were just about to go back upstairs when Mary said, "Hey Paisley, look at this" and pointed to what appeared to be a half-size door just under the upper part of the staircase. I hadn't even noticed that part of the underside of the stairs was closed off since most of them were open to the air below. But this was clearly a storage room, a sort of closet. I immediately thought of Harry Potter and both hoped and dreaded that we might find a small boy living under there.

But when we opened the door, we didn't find a person. Instead, we found a cedar closet, and it was full of leather-bound books, all tucked neatly into shelves and perfectly preserved. "Wow," I whispered."

"Wow is right," Mary said. "These are amazing." She turned to me. "You want them, right?"

"Well, someone needs to have them, so let's take them out and figure out who should keep them. They might belong to someone in the church." Maybe one of the pastors or a member of one of their families had kept diaries, decade's worth it seemed like. I'd have to look at the church history to see who was here long enough to accrue such a collection of writings. If the church granted permission, this would make a great story for my next newsletter.

As we pulled the books out – about four dozen of them – we saw what had preserved them. Behind each set of books on every shelf were small bundles of white chalk tied with twine. They must have used the chalk to absorb moisture, and between that and the cedar, the books were in great shape. The paper and leather alone was gorgeous, and I knew that what-ever was written inside would be priceless, especially to the members of Bethel.

I ran out to the truck and got some of the recycled cardboard boxes I hoarded for situations just like this. We loaded up the books and carted them out. Then, by unspoken mutual agreement, we each took one out and began to read.

My journal started, "May 1908 – Today is sunny, and I should be happy. But I can't help think about what secrets lie buried beneath us, about what we had to hide in order to thrive."

I paused, took a deep breath, and watched Mary. Her eyes were wide, and when she looked at me, I thought she might cry. "Listen," she said and swallowed before she read:

JULY 1910 – *Every day I think of what we have kept buried. Every day, I wonder if I should say something. Every day, I start to tell. But then I can't figure out who to tell because what authority in this town will do anything just with what I say. We are just a bunch of colored folks, the bottom rung of the ladder, and no one but us cares about us. The problem is we have to care about the secrets we keep and the people we keep them about, too, and we don't know how to do that, not in this world, not in the way it is now.*

MARY and I sat quietly for a few minutes on the truck's bumper. I stared at the open journal in my hands and then looked back at the three full boxes of books behind us in the truck. "I guess I know what we're doing for the rest of the day," I said.

She nodded and closed the book in her hands. "I don't think it's wrong to say that we need to know more before we tell anyone, is it?"

I shook my head. "No, right now what we know is that we found a bunch of journals and that the person writing them is struggling with something. That's not enough to really share, though."

"And we don't even know if this is really fact, right? She –

you think it's a she, right?" I nodded – "might be writing a novel or something. Maybe she's inspired by Daphne du Maurier."

I smiled. "Or Henry James. Is it a ghost or not?"

Mary laughed. "Oh, the turn of the screw grows ever tighter." She put her journal back in the box. "Let's get to your place and get reading."

I followed suit, and after we secured the door, locked the house back up, and texted Saul to say we were headed to his lot to unload, we climbed into the cab and drove silently to my new workspace, where we'd left our cars that morning. Fortunately, my son, Sawyer, was with his dad this weekend, so Mary and I could spend the rest of the weekend reading the journals. So by Monday, we could have a plan for what to do and who to tell what.

But first, we needed lunch . . . and reinforcements.

2

When I texted Mika to tell her what we'd found, she offered to have Mrs. Stephenson, her clerk, watch the store so she could come right over. I was grateful because if we needed to stop the demolition of the house, we only had three days — less than three days — to do it. And something told me we would probably need to stop the demolition.

Neither Mary nor I was willing to do that based on a couple of paragraphs of cryptic journals, though. The church had invested a lot of time and money in architectural renderings and site plans for the new addition, and we weren't going to mess that up for just a hint of a reason. For five years, the members had been donating extra money to add on new Sunday School rooms and a Fellowship Hall that would allow them to turn the basement room they'd used for gatherings into a Youth Center. The new kitchen and ADA-accessible bathrooms in the addition would also mean the church could have more weddings and really serve families for funerals. Nope, we had to be sure something merited a pause if we were going to suggest that.

After unloading everything into my space at Saul's construction lot, we shifted the books into my Subaru and then caravanned the few miles east to my farmhouse. The chickens were wandering far and wide in their hunt for the late summer bugs, and I threw them a handful of cracked corn from the lidded steel container I kept by the kitchen door. My small attempts to keep them tame and near home were working, and Sawyer loved picking up our girls and snuggling them close, even after their latest dust bath.

Inside, we put the boxes on the antique trunk I used as a coffee table and set to a crucial piece of business: what we were going to eat. I wasn't what you'd call a foodie, but after recently switching Sawyer and myself to a mainly vegetarian diet to benefit our health and help our food choices align with ones that were good for our earth, I had gotten much pickier about what I'd eat. Mary didn't mind that because she was, herself, a true to the bone foodie and an amazing cook, but Mika had a deep affection for sugar and found my decision to eschew bacon a little disturbing.

Still, we were fortunate to live within delivery distance of a couple of great restaurants that served a variety of food, including amazing black bean burgers, so Mary and I decided to splurge and have food brought in. Business had been pretty good for me of late, and now that I was actually able to contribute to Sawyer's college savings fund, I could stand to go wild by ordering a good meal once in a while.

Our order placed and Mika on her way, Mary and I set up a work station. She began by pulling a small card table out from the storage building behind my house, and I grabbed the TV tray tables from my closet. Then, we arranged space to spread out and put notebooks and pens on each small table so we could make notes of names and dates as needed. I'd been a historian long enough to know that documenting what we

found was crucial if we needed to go back in and find the infor
mation again.

I put out a big pitcher of sweet tea and a bag of dark chocolate candy and confirmed that there was plenty of local hard
cider in the fridge. It was going to be a long afternoon, and why
not enjoy it.

When Mika arrived, we spent a few minutes sorting the
journals by start date and then dividing them into three piles
before we sat down to enjoy our meal and talk through our plan.

After Mary and I caught Mika up on where we'd found the
journals and the little bit we'd read so far, I shared what had
been nagging at me since I'd read the first words in that 1908
journal. "Do you think she means *literally* buried, or is she
talking about some sort of cover-up?"

Mary nodded. "I was wondering the same thing, and my
sense – for what it's worth – is that she's talking literally."

Mika shivered. "Well, that's not creepy at all," she whispered
as she rubbed her hands over her arms.

"Yeah, that's my sense, too." I gathered our empty plates as
Mika took the trash to the can. "Guess we need to find out."

Beverages ready but at a distance from the precious journals, we dove in. I had taken the earliest set of journals since
that's what I'd started reading before. My books dated from
1908 to 1914. Mika had the next span – 1915 to 1921, and Mary
took the final set – 1922 through 1928. We had twenty-one
volumes between us, seven each, and I figured if we read until
we couldn't any longer, we just might make it through the
books by tomorrow evening. I had chosen both sweet tea and
cider to fuel my endeavor, and I wasn't surprised to see my two
best friends had done the same. It was going to be a long day.

I picked up where I left off after making a few notes about
what I needed to know: who was the writer, where was she
based, and what was this secret she was talking about. It didn't

take me long to figure out the second answer. The third entry in
the journal before me read:

WHEN WE MOVED into the manse here next to Bethel, a church
member told us what we had to keep to ourselves about our home,
and now that secret haunts me. I feel guilty every morning when I
wake, and so I spend time here, in the basement, to attend to the
truth, to be close and aware, and to record my frustrations in the
hopes that someone will remember, some day.

I READ that passage aloud to Mika and Mary, and they both
gasped. "So she was in the parish house," Mika said.

"And if she's going to the basement . . ." Mary's voice trailed
off.

"It sure sounds like she's talking about something literally
buried below," I finished as I felt the weight of what we might
be discovering settle more firmly on my shoulders. This could
be a terrible, terrible discovery.

But if I'd learned anything about investigating something
hard from my boyfriend and our county sheriff, Santiago Shifflett, it was best to hold back judgment until we had all the
facts. So I went back to reading, as did Mika and Mary.

From time to time, we each read passages out loud, and as
we went, I made lots of notes. The author was definitely the
pastor's wife, and Mary pulled up the church history on her
phone and confirmed that during those years, the pastor had
been Rev. Fountain Greene, the founding and longest-standing
pastor at Bethel. His wife was named Earnestine, and best we
could tell from the contextual clues, she was the author of these
journals.

She and her husband had moved into the house in May of
1908, right about the time she'd started writing, and her

husband had retired as pastor In 1928, just before the Great Depression descended. So Earnestine's journals spanned her entire time living in the house.

The author and her tie to the manse clear, we plummeted deep to see what we could find about this secret to which she kept referring. References to it were prolific in the first two journal volumes, but as time passed, Earnestine seemed to make peace – or maybe stop thinking about – whatever had bothered her so much when she moved into the house. Over time, she talked more about the people in the community, births and deaths, marriage troubles and children with difficulties. Everything she wrote was compassionate if sometimes very honest, and the more I read, the more I found myself really liking this woman who told it like it was but didn't judge people for their poor choices or past pains.

When dinner time rolled around, I boiled water for pasta, spiced up the jarred spaghetti sauce, and made my quick and easy broiler garlic bread with lots of butter and slices of fresh garlic. Then, I ran out to the garden, harvested the first of the spinach and the lettuce that had managed to survive a Virginia summer without bolting thanks to a shady garden spot, and mixed up a quick green salad. Then, I called my friends to the table for a break, a bottle of wine, and some sustenance. It didn't look like any of us were ready to quit, and with only one or two more journals apiece left to do, we might just be able to finish reading tonight.

Mika helped me set the table, but Mary was absolutely engrossed in whatever she was reading. When she didn't join us after a few minutes, Mika and I picked up all three wine glasses and went back in the living room. The food could wait, and it looked like Beauregard, my gray Maine Coon Cat, was content to sleep with his head on Mary's knee as she continued to read, so our food wasn't in danger from his sometimes pesky paws.

For a few minutes, Mika and I sipped and watched Mary read, glancing at each other with raised eyebrows more than once. Clearly, Mary was intent on finishing, and neither of us dared interrupt.

Finally, just as I was about to get up to pour more wine, Mary closed the journal she was reading, sat back, and said, "Well, we definitely need to adjust our plans for the addition."

I studied her face for a minute and formulated about a million questions, but she still seemed to be considering, weighing what she learned, and I knew she'd share when she had a grasp on what Earnestine's words had revealed. So I sipped what was left in my glass, decided that any more reading I would need to do would have to wait until tomorrow, and felt a bit of pressure ease off. It seemed we had the basic information we needed, if what Mary had learned was as weighty as it seemed, so we could discuss and process a bit before finishing our reading.

After a few more minutes of quiet, Mary said, "There's a Monacan burial mound underneath the manse."

I felt my mouth drop open and stared, unblinking, at my friend as I waited for her to say more.

Mary held up the journal. "In 1928, Earnestine couldn't keep the secret any longer and wrote down all she knew in these pages. Then, she brought up what she knew to the deacons of the church and threatened to go to the newspaper."

"How did the deacons react?" Mika asked in an awed whisper.

"I don't know. Her last entry was written just before she went to the meeting." Mary's face was strained and her jaw tight.

"What?!" I shouted.

Mary sighed. "There's nothing more. That's the last entry." She opened the journal and held it up. As she flipped the pages, I saw no words, only blank paper. She hadn't finished the journal.

"Someone killed her," Mika said.

I turned to look at my friend and shook my head. "We don't know that."

"Well, why else would she stop when she'd kept a journal for twenty-one years?" Mika asked. "What other reason could there be?"

I shook my head again. "I don't know, but we can't jump to conclusions." Dinner forgotten, I grabbed my laptop and opened a genealogy site. I put in the name Earnestine Greene in Octonia, Octonia County, Virginia, and hit search.

It only took a second for the results to return, and I immediately clicked on her death certificate. I scanned the date – August 8, 1928 and looked at Mary. "What's the date of that entry?" I whispered.

Mary flipped back two pages. "August 8, 1928."

I yelped involuntarily and then spun the screen so my friends could see. "She died that day." Both Mika and Mary groaned as I turned the laptop back to me. "It says the cause of death was head trauma, likely from a fall down the stairs." I swallowed the baseball in my throat.

"I think that's pretty clear," Mary said, "but not proof. She could have been so upset that she tripped and fell. Or just missed a step. I've done that."

I sighed. "Yes, that's true. But either way, I think we need to call Santiago. Something horrible happened, and we need him to investigate."

As I told my phone to call my boyfriend, my friends moved the journals back to the boxes, leaving the three that Mika and I still hadn't read out on the table. Then, Mika fixed us each a plate, put all of them on warm in the oven, and finally got out the other bottle of wine. We were going to need it.

. . .

I HADN'T NEEDED to say much on the phone to Santiago. I told him we found something in the parish house at the church and asked if he could come over.

His response had been, "Of course you did, and of course I'll be right over." This was the fourth time one of my salvaging expeditions had required police involvement, and while I was grateful that I had met Santiago through one of those situations, I hated that now I had to call him for something other than an invitation to sit on the porch and talk.

While we waited for the sheriff, Mika and Mary tidied up the living room and stacked all our notes together to review after we ate, and I texted Sawyer's dad to see if I could video chat with our son for a minute. My son always pulled me back to a place of perspective, and while I didn't rely on my son to be my support, tonight, I did want to see his face, to be reminded that he was okay.

His dad readily agreed, as eager as I was on the nights he was with me to have a little support in caring for this wild, rambunctious, amazing little boy. Sawyer and I talked a bit while he splashed like a seal in his kiddie pool. That boy loved water, and it always gave me joy to see him freely doing what he adored. But as usual, his attention span for the phone was limited, and so I said goodnight, feeling good that he was okay. When we hung up, I felt a little more balanced.

By the time Santiago arrived, Mary, Mika, and I were into our first glass of the second bottle of wine, but the alcohol and time together seemed to have steadied us all. So when Santiago sat down with a heaping plate of spaghetti, warm garlic bread, and a salad, we were ready to talk.

Mary explained what she'd read, and I told him what I'd seen in Earnestine's death certificate. And Mika asked Santiago what he thought had happened to her.

"Her death is certainly suspicious," he said, "but we can't jump to any conclusions until we know more."

Mika laughed. "That's exactly what Paisley said."

Santiago squeezed my hand on the table. "You're learning."

I smiled. "I am, but between us, we can admit this is in the *highly* suspicious category, right?"

He rolled his eyes but smiled. "Sure, if that makes you feel better. I'll even use the phrase 'highly suspicious' when I tell Savannah." Savannah Winslow was Santiago's deputy, and she had become a friend over the past few months.

"Please do," I said, trying to keep the tone light. But the situation was too heavy for my efforts, and I gave up. "And what do we do about the possibility that there are Native American graves under the house?"

A collective sigh passed around the table. "I know a professor at UVA. We can talk with him," Santiago said. "He'll keep things quiet because he doesn't want more graves disturbed, but he can also guide us on what to do."

I nodded. "Okay. Can I come with you when you talk to him? I feel responsible since it was my work that brought all this to light."

"Sure. Let me reach out to him tonight and see if he might be free tomorrow, okay?" He squeezed my hand again, and I tried to smile.

"That's good because I need to tell the deacon board what's happening ASAP so we can stop the heavy machinery from coming in if need be. I'd like to be able to give them a recommendation for next steps," Mary said as she pushed her uneaten spaghetti around her plate.

I looked at my friend, and the sadness of this information and, I suspected, the fact that the church's hard work to build their much-needed addition would have to be put on hold, maybe permanently, showed on her face. "I'm sorry, Mary."

Mika reached over and squeezed her shoulders. "Would it be alright with you if I let Saul know that we have a situation –

no details – so that his crew is prepared if they aren't needed
Monday?"

Mary looked at Mika and sighed. "Sure. That's probably
wise."

"And let me also talk to him about his friend who is an
architect. Maybe we can work some magic with the plans you
already have and find a way to get that addition without
disrupting anyone's eternal rest," Mika added.

"Okay. But it seems impossible. Our cemetery is on the
other side of the church, and we don't own the lot behind us."
She wrapped her fingers around the back of her neck. "But the
Lord can make a way where it seems there is no way." She
smiled over at Mika.

"That's the attitude," Santiago said. "I'll go call Dr. Harmon
now." He looked down at his plate before he stood. "The food
was really good Paisley, just . . ."

None of us had eaten much except the garlic bread. Clearly,
we had needed comfort food in the form of carbs and butter.
"No worries at all. The chickens will feast well tonight." That
was one of the best perks about these silly birds. They would
eat anything, and I never had to waste food.

Just as I was about to scrape the last dish onto mine to carry
outside, I felt a fluffy tail wrap around my ankles. "What is it,
Beau? Do you think you want some spaghetti?"

He mewled and continued to weave around my legs. "Oh, I
see. You want bread." I dropped a crust onto the floor for him
and watched him lick it carefully before picking it up in his
front teeth and carrying it to who knows where to eat. For a
giant cat, he was so persnickety.

The chickens went right to work on the mound of spaghetti,
and after I filled their feeder and checked their water, I penned
them into their electric fence so that they'd be safe as the night
predators began to come out. I'd close them in their coop at
dark, but raccoons sometimes started their hunting raids early.

Back inside, Mary and Mika were quietly loading the dish washer, and I could hear Santiago on the phone out on the front porch. I took a wet cloth and wiped the table and let myself, for the first time, think about what it mean to have a burial ground very close to downtown Octonia. People would likely want to both make it a tourist attraction and resent that idea, but given the very little I knew about Monacan burial mounds here in the area, I thought it was probably something the Monacan people themselves would want to keep more quiet. Grave robberies were sadly still common because some folks seemed to be unable to think of Native Americans as people. I'd heard more than one Monacan leader give an interview where they suggested people consider what it would be like if someone opened Grandma's grave to steal her favorite pearls.

The kitchen clean and the wine still flowing, we three women returned to the living room with our notes. We talked through what we'd learned and saw that, unsurprisingly, many of the families mentioned in Earnestine Greene's journals were still members at Bethel. Mary recognized many of the people in the journals, too, had even known a few of the folks in their later years. "It's a family church," she said. "People have really close ties to it."

I nodded. In the research I'd done so far on the church, I'd learned that it was founded after a split from another nearby church, something about the practices of baptism. The members of Bethel had built their church on land someone gave them for that purpose.

Mary and I had been wanting to find out who the donor had been, but the church records were oddly silent on the subject. I wondered, out loud, if I could write up some of the church history for my newsletter and see if anyone knew anything."

Mary shrugged. "Sure. I don't know that most people care

about this stuff, and the young people almost certainly don't," Mary said with a sigh. "Now, if you can put your story to a good beat . . ." She laughed.

"No one wants to hear Paisley beatbox," Mika said. "Trust me."

We then talked about our most embarrassing moments in a conversation spurred by Mika telling Mary about how I had wanted to perform "Rapper's Delight" at our college talent show but had forgotten both the words and the rhythm on stage. It had been mortifying.

Mary was just about to give us details about the time she flashed an entire highway when Santiago came in. We immediately grew silent and stared at him.

"Dr. Harmon is eager to meet with us bright and early tomorrow, and he'd like to see the journals," Santiago turned to Mary, "if that's okay."

"It's just fine, of course. This is the one where Earnestine talks about the burial ground, but of course, he can read them all if he'd like." Mary handed Santiago the leather-bound journal.

"I'll let him know, but for now, I think this is enough. That said, if you guys want to read the last of these, it might be good to get that done tonight since it's possible I will need to take these into evidence if we find information about a crime." Santiago's face looked strained. This was going to be a huge deal if it turned out that people were buried under the manse and if someone had been killed to keep that a secret.

"Let's read then, women," I said and picked up the final journal from my stack while Mika handed Mary one from hers.

"Do you mind if I look at your notes?" Santiago asked. "I need to start getting familiar with the names and facts here."

I handed him the stack of paper, and then, we all began to read. Now that we knew Earnestine's handwriting and were pretty familiar with the kind of things she wrote about, we made quick work of the remaining three books, only adding a few names and a couple of events to our notes. It was clear that Mary had found the crucial information in her reading, and while the other pieces of data might help once we knew more, for now, we'd done all we could.

"I'm going to call Saul now," Mika said and stepped into the kitchen.

I looked over at Mary. "You're welcome to stay here tonight, sleep in Sawyer's room, come with us in the morning."

Mary smiled. "Actually, I'd like that, if you don't mind another tagalong, Santiago."

"I think that would be really helpful, Mary. You know more about the church history than anyone, and I expect you'll be able to answer a lot of Dr. Harmon's questions."

"Maybe," she said, "but probably not the crucial one. How could anyone allow a house to be built on the top of a cemetery?"

3

When I was six, my mom made a terrible slip in judgment at the prompting of another parent and gave the okay for me to watch the movie *Poltergeist*. The other mom had said it was actually pretty funny, but I had nightmares about people coming up from the ground for weeks. The only thing that had calmed me was for Mom to remind me that God puts a hedge of protection around us and to assure me that it stretched out "even on the bottom."

That night, as Mary slept under Sawyer's spaceship sheets, those nightmares came back, except this time the horror wasn't that I would be attacked but that I wouldn't be able to help. I just kept seeing those people reaching up through the ground, and I couldn't move to save them or even hear them. I woke in a cold sweat.

Since I couldn't possibly go back to sleep, I got up, made coffee, and sat down on the couch with Beauregard to cross-stitch. I was working on a very simple red bulldozer to give to Sawyer at Christmas, and the fact that I only had to use one shade of red thread on the boxy pattern was immensely soothing. I counted and stitched until my strands ran out. Then, I rethreaded and began again.

Typically, I liked harder patterns, ones that involve multiple colors and blended threads, maybe even some metallics for flare, but this morning I was grateful for simple and clear. The in and out of the needle soothed my mind, and by the time I needed to shower to get ready for our meeting with Dr. Harmon, I was feeling much better.

As I finished getting ready, Mary woke and came down the stairs. "That bed is super comfortable," she said. "I haven't slept that well in a while."

"Wow, well maybe I'll just give Saw my bed and get into that one. If you slept well after all the news yesterday, that must be a miracle mattress." I stepped out of the bathroom and pointed to the small table in the corner. "I left some towels here, and use anything in the shower you want . . . if you want to shower."

She nodded and gave me a quick hug as I stepped around her and headed to make breakfast. I decided we needed good sustenance and protein for the long morning ahead, so I whipped up scrambled eggs with extra sharp cheddar and popped some bread into the oven for avocado toast. When I had first seen the mention of avocado toast on *Fixer Upper* I had scoffed. It seemed weird and trendy; wasn't guacamole good enough?

But then, I'd tried it with some feta on a piece of bread, and I was hooked. It was delicious. Now, it was a staple for most breakfasts in my house, even though avocados weren't local and sort of broke my loose rule about not having food shipped thousands of miles. I made an exception for avocado toast, though.

When Mary came out of the bathroom looking fresh and vibrant, I placed a plate of eggs and toast in front of her and poured her some strong, dark coffee with cream but not sugar, just like she liked it. She threw back her head and laughed.

"Watch out. I may be staying at Chez Sutton all the time now. Between the bed and the breakfast, this is pretty sweet."

"Anytime. Sawyer eschews his bed, so it's always free . . . and when he's here, maybe you can convince him to try a bite of avocado," I said with a smile.

"I do have a magical way with children," she said, chuckling. But she wasn't exaggerating. Mary lost her own son to cancer when he was fourteen. But despite that grief, she taught Sunday School and helped in the nursery at church, and after services children held onto her legs like she was Santa Claus. They adored her . . . and so did my son. Auntie Mary was one of his favorite people, along with Santiago and his police car.

The two of us ate in relative quiet, each catching up on the world through our phones until we heard Santiago pull in the driveway. He'd brought his 1980s-something pickup, and I loved it. But not for a ride into Charlottesville. I valued my spine health too much for that. We'd be taking my car, rock-hard fruit snacks and all.

Before Santiago could even knock, the two of us were out the door, leaving Beauregard to stare longingly after us. I often took him with me on trips because he loved to ride and he walked well on a leash, but I didn't think taking him to visit a university was exactly appropriate this morning. I'd make it up to him with fresh tuna later.

I pointed to my car as Santiago greeted us, and he turned on his heel and made it to my door before I did, opening it for me with a flourish. He wasn't one of those men who stood on chivalry as his highest virtue, and for that I was glad . . . but I was also glad when he did little things to take care of me, too.

When he insisted that Mary sit up front, I smiled, but Mary protested until finally he climbed into the seat behind me, shut the door, and buckled his seat belt. Mary rolled her eyes and then climbed in next to me. "Don't worry. His stubbornness landed him in a seat that might not be quite dry from Friday's chocolate milk incident," I said.

Santiago lifted himself out of the seat and then said, "Glad I wore dark pants" as he laughed.

The drive to the university usually took about forty-five minutes simply because of traffic once you got close to town. But on an early Sunday morning, the roads were clear, the lights in our favor, and the drive quite fun since Mary insisted that we go back to our teenage years and listen to the classic rock station. I was still coming to terms that the music I'd listened to in high school and college was "classic" now, but when Rick Astley's "Never Gonna Give You Up" came on I didn't hesitate to sing along, even though I knew I was Rick-rolling myself.

Dr. Harmon's office was in a stately brick building near the Rotunda at the center of campus, which UVA refers to as "the Grounds". He'd told Santiago that he'd meet us on the front steps to let us in because the building was locked up for the weekend. I hadn't been in this or many buildings at the university since I hadn't attended here and didn't spend a lot of time in the area. But the Grounds were beautiful with big old trees, crisscrossing sidewalks, two-hundred-year-old buildings. It was what I always thought of when someone used the word *university*.

When we reached the steps, a slight, graying man with fair skin was waiting for us. He had on sneakers, a baseball cap, and a T-shirt that said, "Make My Day" in bright yellow letters across the front. I liked him immediately.

We said our greetings, and then he led us up two flights of stairs to his office, which was a lovely space with natural light, a collection of shadowboxes full of arrowheads (which he would tell me were more appropriately called "projectile points"), and bookshelves stretching from floor to ceiling. In the center of the

room sat a majestic desk with huge feet that looked like it
might have killed the people who had to carry it up here.

Dr. Harmon had gathered chairs for us, and we all sat down
and got right to it when he asked to see the journal Mary was
carrying. On the way over, she had slipped some old ribbon I
had in the car into the seams by the appropriate pages, so the
professor was able to read through what she'd found quite
quickly.

"Well, this is fascinating," he said, "and disturbing, of
course." He leaned back in his chair and studied Mary's face.
"I'm sorry you have inherited this history at your church. It is
not your fault, but of course, it is now your responsibility."

Without hesitation, Mary said, "Absolutely, and I will do all
I can to do right by the people involved in this story." She
glanced over at me. "And I know Paisley will too."

"Of course. That's part of why we are here. We need to know
what to do, and Santiago thought you might be able to give us
some guidance." I found my voice surprisingly choked with
emotion.

Santiago, who was always compassionate but also able to
maintain his equilibrium a little better than I was, added, "Do
you think it's possible that there are Monacan graves under that
building?"

Dr. Harmon stood and walked toward his desk, where he
picked up a road atlas and brought it back to where we were
sitting. "Let me show you a bit about where the Monacans lived
and often placed their burial grounds."

He first located Octonia and then said, "Between these two
rivers, the Fleur and the Skonset, are some of the ancestral
homelands of the Monacan people, although the Monacans
had settlements and traveled to hunt and trade throughout this
area. Historically, they built their villages along waterways and
had their burial mounds a bit away from water."

I leaned closer and studied the map. The church and parish

house were almost equidistant from the two rivers, and given that they sat on a slight hill, it made sense to me, with what little I knew, that people might choose to bury their loved ones there. "So it's possible?"

"Possible. Probable even," Dr. Harmon said. "We don't reveal where burial mounds are specifically anymore because people then visit them as tourist sites."

"And because I suspect people rob them, too," Santiago added.

Dr. Harmon nodded grimly. "Exactly. But I can tell you that there is another burial mound not far from this location, so I'd say that it would be very wise and historically just to take these claims that this woman is making very seriously and do some more research."

I nodded. "Thank you," I said.

Mary added, "Yes, thank you, and I assure you we will take this all very seriously. I give you my word."

Dr. Harmon smiled. "Would you like me to introduce you to the chief of the Monacan Nation? I'm sure she would be eager to talk with you and work with you to discover more."

A smile lit Mary's face. "I would like that very much. If you don't mind making that introduction, I'd love to have her – and you if you'd like to come – to the church so we could do some preliminary looks at the site."

Santiago looked at me and gave me a thin smile. "Looks like they'll have a delay in the demo, and rightly so. Did you get all the things you wanted from the house already?"

"I did," I said and then turned to Dr. Harmon. "I do architectural salvage, and this is one of my sites."

"How fascinating." Dr. Harmon asked. "I bet you find the most interesting things."

"I do. That's how we came to find these journals actually." I looked back at Santiago. "A delay is just fine if we do right by these people buried here. I know Saul will agree."

"Agreed," Mary said. "Let's call Saul right away and let him know that we're on an indefinite hold, and I'll get the deacon board together right away."

We stood, and each of us shook Dr. Harmon's hand. "Whenever the chief wants to come out, I will make myself available," Mary said. "This is now my top priority."

"Thank you very much, and I know Chief Stephenson will be eager to come out. I'll be in touch as soon as I know," he said as he walked us to the door. "Sheriff Shifflett, can you send me everyone's numbers?"

Santiago took out his phone and tapped the screen. "Done."

As the three of us walked back down the stairs and let ourselves out of the building, I felt a twist of anticipation in my stomach. This situation was potentially horrible, an act of the worst levels of disrespect and prejudice possible, and moving through these next few days was not going to be easy for any of us. But still, it felt good, exciting even, to be able to be part of righting a historical harm.

THE RIDE HOME was a quiet one. As Santiago drove, Mary and I sent dozens of text messages and answered the responding phone calls to give more details. By the time we pulled back up at my house, Mary had a plan to meet the deacon board right after the church service and there was a visit with Chief Stephenson and Dr. Harmon planned for three p.m. I had already let Saul know to move his crew to other jobs for the first part of week, and I was going to accompany Santiago to the site to hang police tape and cordon off the building and the immediate surrounding yard.

This was something Deputy Winslow would typically do, and Santiago had kept her up to speed. But since there was no real police work to be done and it was Sunday, he decided it would be fine for me to help with this small thing and let

Savannah enjoy the rest of her day off. "She'll have a busy enough week ahead anyway," he said. "Besides, it'll give me a chance to pay my own respects to the people there."

"We don't know for sure anyone is buried there," I said, hearing the incredulity in my voice even as I spoke. "I mean, I think people are buried there, and we need to treat it with respect. But it wouldn't be wise to presume anything."

Mary sighed. "Exactly. We need to act as if, but also not spread any rumors."

"Agreed," Santiago said as Mary walked toward her car. "So nothing to anyone who doesn't already know, right?"

Mary and I both nodded. "The word will spread fast enough as it is," Mary said.

I feared she was right. People in Octonia were hungry for news, and bad news burned through our community like a dynamite fuse. I wanted to be optimistic, but I expected the word would be out by late afternoon at the earliest. I could only hope that the church could put a plan of action together before people started asking questions.

ONCE MARY WAS on her way to make copies of the journal pages for the deacon board and prepare her presentation for them — a presentation that she hoped would make them at least pause the demo and construction plans without any outside intervention, Santiago and I sat down on the porch with a fresh pot of coffee.

"Not exactly what I expected when I was popping baseboards off twenty-four hours ago," I said quietly.

"I imagine not, but you did the right thing when you found those journals, Paisley. It would have been easier to just cover things up, pretend you hadn't read anything." Santiago said as he took my hand. "But you are not someone who does easy when easy is wrong."

I smiled. "Sometimes I wish I was though. I don't want to be that way, but I totally get why people tout 'leave the past in the past.' Pulling the legacies of history into the light of now isn't always pleasant work."

"No. No, it's not." He took a long swig of his black coffee and rocked in his chair for a few moments. "Did you tell Mika the latest?"

I nodded. "I texted her on the way home. She's at the shop today but offered to close up early if we needed help."

"That was kind of her, but I think you and I can handle what we need to do." He stood and helped me to my feet. "You ready?"

I finished my coffee and nodded. "Yep." We put our mugs in the dishwasher and then got into Santiago's cruiser for the drive back into town.

As we parked at the back of the lot, I could hear the congregation singing inside, and a pang of longing went through my chest. I wanted to join them, but I knew that wasn't wise, not today when I might not be able to keep myself from talking about what we'd found. I wanted to give Chief Stephenson and the deacon board a chance to consider the situation first before people started asking a lot of questions.

So while the strains of "A Mighty Fortress" wafted through the sanctuary walls, Santiago and I wrapped bright yellow tape all around the house and the fence without saying a word. I knew that in some ways this action shouted that something was going on, but we needed to be sure we were doing our best to protect the resting place of the people who might be buried here, even if it might draw more curiosity than we wanted. We needed to keep people out, and we needed Chief Stephenson to see we were doing our best to respect the assumed graves of her people.

Fortunately, we finished long before the service let out so we were able to move the cruiser down the street and wait for

Mary. I'd told her we'd be available if she wanted us at the deacon meeting, and Santiago was eager to be on hand if people had questions about the legalities involved. While we waited, he called a contact at the Department of Historic Resources in Richmond, apologized for disturbing her Sunday, and then explained the situation. She said we were taking the right action and that she'd be out at three to hear what the chief wanted us to do and to give legal guidance about next steps.

I was glad she was coming, but this situation felt like it was getting bigger and bigger very quickly. For a brief moment, I wondered if we were taking things too far, and then I thought about what I would think if someone built a house over the cemetery where my mother was buried. The rage that sparked in me at just the idea reminded me that we were taking appropriate action, that we needed to do everything we could to find the truth and protect the people buried here — if we found out there were graves.

For a moment or two, Santiago and I tried to chat about Sawyer and other lighter things, but soon, the weight of the situation settled onto us with silence. I put my head against the car seat and watched the sun dance in the trees above.

After a few anxious minutes, Mary texted and asked us to join her for the meeting. "They're singing the final hymn now, so if you want to come in the back, you can avoid most folks."

Santiago and I made our way up the wheelchair ramp at the side of the building and slipped into the side door that led to the back entrance to the sanctuary and the Sunday School rooms behind it. We found Mary in the largest classroom and joined her in the circle of folding chairs that lined the room.

She was wringing her hands in her lap, and beside her on a small table, she had Earnestine's journal and stacks of paper. "Thanks for coming," she said.

I reached over and took her hand. "Of course. We're here to

support you, so you just let us know what you need when you need it."

She nodded. "Santiago, maybe you can be prepared to explain what it means for something to be a crime scene?"

"Definitely. Just let me know when." He smiled and straightened his uniform. He was ready, as usual. I knew that his work wore on him sometimes, but in moments like this, he was confident in his ability to do his job well. It was an attractive trait for sure.

While we waited for everyone to join us, Mary went over what she was going to share, showed us the pages of Earnestine's journal she had copied to distribute, and asked us if we thought she should mention anything else. Santiago told her about the Department of Historic Resources rep coming this afternoon, and she jotted that down on her notes. "That's good," she said. "I think most people here will be on the same page, but we have spent a lot of money and time on this addition. It's going to be a blow that we have to stop work for a bit."

I nodded. "I totally get that, but hopefully everyone will understand." I wasn't sure they all would, but I wanted to reassure my friend, give her a boost of confidence.

The doors to the sanctuary swung open, and I could hear the organist playing his postlude, a lively rendition of "Great Is Thy Faithfulness." I said a silent prayer for understanding and cooperation, and then braced myself for a hard hour.

After everyone was seated, Mary did an excellent job of recounting the events of yesterday, of explaining why we needed to halt all the plans, and suggesting a course of action moving forward. Then, before allowing anyone else to speak – and a lot of people had something to say – she asked Santiago to inform them about the status of the house site.

"It's an active crime scene," he said, "so as you can expect, we need to keep it closed to everyone except those who need access to evaluate the grounds and study the situation. I know you understand."

Several of the individuals who had been sitting forward ready to weigh in sat back and nodded. But one man didn't wait half a second until after Santiago finished before he said, "I need to say something here."

He was very polished in a fine, three-piece suit and the shiniest dress shoes I'd ever seen. His haircut was crisp and tight to his head, and he had on gold-rimmed glasses that were the perfect complement to his walnut-colored skin. This man looked like he was used to commanding a room.

I braced myself, ready for him to set into the run-down on what the church had gone through to raise the funds and make the plans, but instead, he said, "My family's graves were plowed through over near Chestnut Heights Plantation. I will never know where they were buried. Because they were slaves, no one marked their graves, no one honored their resting place, and no one respected their lives. We cannot let that happen to anyone who might be buried on ground that we own."

Mary scribbled on her notepad and turned it slightly toward me. "Demetrius Cleveland, chair," her note said.

"I'm glad to hear you say that, Demetrius, because I completely agree. I think a lot of us will never know the final resting place of our people because of slavery and Jim Crow. The least we can do here is pass along the honor and respect we wish our ancestors had been given," Mary said.

Almost every head at the table nodded, and I felt a weight lift. We were, it seemed, in agreement. Now, I felt like I could speak. "I've also asked a friend to consult with an architect to see if, need be, the addition could be accommodated in some other way. He's donating that consultation fee to the church." I knew Saul would not be asking for any payment, so I felt confident making that assurance.

"Good. Thank you," Chairman Cleveland said with a nod to me, "So let's vote. Do I have a motion?"

One woman in a fine purple hat said, "I move that we halt any further action on the proposed church addition, including demolition of the existing manse, until a complete and full study of the site, its history, and the presence of any burials can be conducted."

I was impressed. She had succinctly and professionally summarized just what Mary had suggested, and a man across the table seconded her motion without hesitation.

When Chairman Cleveland called for the vote, it was unanimous, and Mary audibly sighed when the motion passed and the meeting was adjourned.

As everyone started to get up and go about their day, Santiago said, "There is crime scene tape around the building now because we all know this is going to be news on the gossip train here in town. Would you all mind calling if you see someone on site who isn't authorized?"

Many of the church members lived on this same block, including Mary, so they would be the best alarm system Santiago could employ.

Several people spoke up and said they would, and then, everyone but Demetrius Cleveland headed toward their cars and, I suspected, some really good food. As my stomach growled, I felt a pang of regret that I wouldn't be having my usual lunch at Mary's house today. Her pot roast was out of this world.

"How can I help?" Chairman Cleveland asked Mary as we all milled around the table, not sure what to do next.

Mary smiled. "You did a lot this morning, Demetrius. Thank you. Would you like to join us this afternoon at three?"

"I would like that," he said, "and let me introduce myself, Paisley. I've seen you at services but haven't made a point of meeting you. I apologize. Demetrius Cleveland." He put out his hand and gave mine a firm shake.

"It's nice to meet you," I said with a smile. "Now, if it's not too forward and selfish, could we all go get some lunch before our next meeting?"

Demetrius clapped me on the back. "I knew I liked you," he said. "My treat for burgers at the Pierce Inn?" he asked.

I smiled. "Did you say burgers?" Their veggie burger was incredible, and I made it a habit to never pass up a free lunch.

We all laughed and headed to the historic inn up the street.

4

The chef at the Pierce Inn was a Michelin-star rated superstar, but he also respected his local setting and served up the most amazing burgers alongside the more formal fare.

As we walked the couple of blocks to Main Street, I texted Mika to let her know things had gone well and that I'd keep her posted. She answered immediately, "Great. Busy day here, which is good, but sorry I can't join you."

I sent her three smiley emojis and tuned back to the conversation around me. Demetrius was telling us about how he'd come to know where his ancestors on his mother's side had been enslaved and how much easier it had been to find his father's family since they were all free people of color. "I mean they were still tracked like property, but at least they had some legal standing."

I knew just what he meant. I'd done a little genealogical research for some families related to the buildings I'd salvaged from, and it was really hard to find anything about enslaved people at all. "So have you been to Chestnut Ridge?" I asked.

"Not yet, but the new owners have invited my family over. They're really open to sharing what information they have and learning more about our family," Demetrius said.

"That's refreshing," Mary said. "Sometimes these folks aren't interested at all, too afraid we'll up and claim the plantation as our own."

"And right you could," I said. "Those places are black places far more than white places if you go back to the sheer numbers of people who have lived there."

"A woman who appreciates food and speaks the truth," Demetrius said with a laugh. "We are going to be fast friends."

Santiago smiled and quickly squeezed my hand. "She is a charmer, this one," he said.

Demetrius glanced at our clasped hands and gently said, "I'm glad she found someone who appreciates her."

The host seated us quickly at a table with a view of the mountains beyond, and within minutes, we had our orders in – burgers for everyone, although Demetrius got the black bean burger with extra cheese because he was trying to eat a plant-based diet, he said. "Can't go without the cheese, though."

I echoed his earlier words. "I knew I liked you."

His wonderful laugh bounced around the room, and when Santiago joined him, I realized that this man's confidence and kindness were just what we needed as we prepared for hard conversations and the truth of historical trauma this afternoon.

"So what are we sharing with Chief Stephenson? Did you say that was her name?" Demetrius asked.

"Right," Mary answered. "I expect Dr. Harmon will have told her everything we know, so I'm much more interested in what she wants to do. She might want archaeology done, she might not. And I'm not sure whether she'll think it better to leave the house standing or take it down. I'm hoping we can simply hear what she has to say and do our best to honor it as we move along in next steps to discover if this is indeed a burial ground."

Demetrius nodded. "I like that plan, and what about Earnestine? It sounds like you all think she might have been murdered for what she told our predecessors."

Mary glanced at me, and I nodded. "It sounds like it, and if it's okay with you all, I'd be happy to look into that. See what I can find in the papers, do a little historical research to see if we can find out more. Would that be okay?"

Demetrius nodded. "That would be excellent. We need to understand her story, too, even as we work to figure out the Monacan ties to our church."

"I'll get started right away," I said as I eyed the juicy veggie burger with onion rings and barbecue sauce that the waitress slid in front of me. "After I eat this burger of course."

"And Paisley, maybe you can write about Earnestine in your newsletter, give her a little homage about what you find," Mary suggested.

I smiled. "I'd love that, but of course, I'll run anything by you. I want to be sure what I write is accurate but also appropriate in terms of the church's history and mission."

"Thanks for that," Demetrius said as he picked up his burger. "Now, Sheriff, tell me the latest news about town."

From there, the conversation veered to talk about the new housing development that was still in discussions at the edge of town, the recent interest in skateboarding that had meant teenagers were using the mostly empty library parking lot to do their tricks, and the sheriff's offices latest efforts to help support a local community effort to create a robust after-school program.

I listened to Santiago share things I already knew and let myself simply admire him for how good he was at his job. This afternoon was going to be tough, and it was nice to escape into the daily for just a little bit while I enjoyed some amazing food.

Soon, though, we needed to head back to open up the parish house and prepare for the Chief's arrival. So Demetrius paid our bill and received sincere thanks from the rest of us before we made a quiet walk back to the church. When we arrived, the parking lot was full, and we all exchanged looks of concern. It seemed the rumor mill had already begun.

But I couldn't see anyone near the manse itself, so Mary stepped into the church to see what was going on. A few moments later, she returned to join us on the house porch and said, "The congregation is inside praying."

Tears sprung to my eyes. "For this meeting?"

Mary nodded and swallowed. "For us."

"We are good people," Demetrius said and then followed Santiago under the police tape and through the front door.

By tacit agreement, we all waited at the front door. No one wanted to stand outside in the sun and where the passing cars might wonder about a group lingering far more than a full parking lot, given how the church was a usual gathering places for all sorts of events and groups. It was just before three, and I expected no one would be late.

I was right. At exactly three, two cars pulled into the lot, and three people stepped out. I expected the woman in the suit to be the DHR representative, and I wasn't wrong. She introduced herself as Eliza Dixon when she came in.

Dr. Harmon walked beside an older woman in a long shift dress toward the building.

"Chief Stephenson," Mary greeted her as soon as they came in to join us. "Thank you for coming. I wish it could be under more pleasant circumstances."

"Believe it or not, as hard as this is, I am glad to be here, glad you have moved kindly and quickly. So in that sense, this is pleasant." Her voice was soft but clear, and I recognized the voice of a woman who expected honor and didn't have to manipulate to get attention or respect. I was impressed.

"Could you please show me to the basement?" she asked. "I understand it has a dirt floor, and if my ancestors are here, I want to pay them respect first thing."

Mary nodded. "Of course," she said and led the way down the creaky steps. Once we were all there, Chief Stephenson knelt to the ground, placed her palms down, and grew silent. We stood, heads bowed around her, until she rose again.

"Thank you," she said. "Now, may I see the journal?"

"Absolutely. It's upstairs." She turned to me. "Paisley, do you mind getting us some chairs from the fellowship hall?"

"Sure thing," I said.

"I'll help," Santiago said as he and Demetrius followed me across the parking lot to the backdoor and down into the basement below the sanctuary. We grabbed six chairs from the rack at the edge of the room and made our way back to set them up in the front parlor of the house.

Once we were all seated, Chief Stephenson opened up the journal to the pages Mary had marked and read. Tears sprung to her eyes at one point, but she didn't stop reading. Then, she looked up and said, "Thank you."

For a few moments, we all sat in silence, allowing the chief to gather her thoughts and lead the conversation. I don't know what I expected her to say, but I was completely surprised when she began with, "How are you honoring Ms. Earnestine's sacrifice?"

I sighed. "I am going to research her life, see what else I can find out about her, write about her."

"Good," she said, "because she was murdered, don't we think?"

Everyone around the room except Ms. Dixon nodded. "Murdered?" she asked.

"Earnestine's journal ends on the day she says she is going to tell the church leadership about the burial ground," Mary said as she looked at Santiago. "We don't know for sure, but yes, we think she might have been killed."

"People have been murdered for exposing less onerous forms of truth," Chief Stephenson said with a weight of knowing that felt palpable. "I'm glad you are looking into her life and death."

Demetrius asked, "And how would you like us to proceed to determine if your ancestors are buried here?"

Chief Stephenson smiled. "I appreciate that question and the steps you have already taken on the presumption that they are. I assure you that this is a burial ground. After I received Dr. Harmon's call this morning, I went into the scant records we have, and I was, well — *pleased* isn't exactly the right word — heartened to find that we have records showing people as buried here in Octonia. No exact spot is noted, but I feel it is far too much of a coincidence to say this isn't their resting place."

I took a deep breath. I agreed with her, but my voice in this conversation was not important. So I simply nodded.

"Agreed," Demetrius said. "We will operate with this certainty then." I felt a finality of the situation sink into the room, but it appeared everyone, even Ms. Dixon agreed.

"I will file a formal report tomorrow then. While I'm here, I'll georeference the location of the house to our cemeteries map, and by tomorrow afternoon, this ground will be marked as sacred and therefore protected from any further disturbance."

"Thank you," Chief Stephenson said again, and I couldn't help but think it odd that she was thanking us for trying to restore something that never should have been destroyed in the first place.

"How would you like us to handle the house? It was slated to be demolished starting Tuesday." Mary said.

Chief Stephenson paused and seemed to think for a

moment. "I pondered that thought all the way over the mountain today, and I think we would like for it to be removed. I will confirm that with the Tribal Council tonight, but yes, I think we would like to be able to visit their graves without the house between us, especially since the church had plans to take down the building anyway."

"Then once you confirm, we will proceed," Demetrius said.

"And the Nation will split the expense of doing so with you," Chief Stephenson said.

"Respectfully, I must decline. Please let us do this act of reparation for you. We would want the same for our ancestors."

Chief Stephenson smiled and inclined her head. "Very well. Let me talk to the Council, and we can proceed if, as I suspect, they agree with this plan."

With the beginnings of a plan in mind, we stood and headed back outside to talk while Ms. Dixon used her phone to walk the perimeter of the manse yard and then the church itself.

While Demetrius and Dr. Harmon talked about the church's history, I approached Chief Stephenson. "Chief Stephenson, would you mind if I researched the history of this land after your people were here? See if I can figure out how this terrible situation came to be?"

"Please call me Amanda, and yes, that would be wonderful. It seems unlikely that someone didn't know something at some point."

I smiled. "I hope so. I'll let Dr. Harmon know what I find?"

"Or just email me." She took a business card out of her bag. "I'm an internet junky."

WHEN WE LEFT THE CHURCHYARD, the members were still inside praying, and something about that felt powerful, strong. I wasn't sure how I thought prayer worked, but the fact that dozens of people were taking the time to think about this hard, hard situation gave me a lot of hope. For the first time since yesterday morning, I felt joy bump around in my chest.

Santiago and I chatted about what we were going to do next as he drove me home, and while I knew all of this was a huge deal for him professionally, he also seemed a little lighter, a little more optimistic.

"I'm off shift in about thirty minutes, so would it be awkward if I stayed at your place for a few hours and did some research while you did yours?" he asked.

"I'd love that," I said and meant it. One of the things I'd always enjoyed most about college was the way that you could be with someone – reading, researching, writing – but not have to talk. That kind of companionship was always energizing to me. "Would it be most helpful to you if I started with Earnestine's history?"

He nodded. "I think so. That's the actual potential murder involved here. The violation of sacred burial grounds is illegal, too, but given that the person who committed that crime is probably long dead, I think it's best to focus on the crime we might be able to prosecute."

"Makes sense to me," I said as we pulled into my driveway. "Sawyer is coming home in a couple of hours, so let's make the most of this time. I'll put in a frozen pizza, and then we can play with him before he goes to bed. Sound okay?"

"Perfect," Santiago said, and I felt my heart get a little gooey at this man who didn't hesitate to interrupt his plans for a preschooler. He grabbed a bag from the back of his car and followed me inside.

As he set up his laptop on the dining room table, I grabbed mine from my office and did the same. Soon, we were both typing and reading, scribbling notes and sharing interesting bits of information with each other.

I had begun my search with Earnestine Greene's name on

the genealogy website I used most often. I knew her husband was Fountain, and so I was able to find her pretty quickly in census records. Her death certificate was also available, and she did, indeed, die in August of 1928.

I interrupted Santiago to read him the cause of death. "Head trauma caused by a fall," the document read.

"Well, that only lends credence to the possibility that someone killed her," Santiago said with a frown.

I nodded. "Yeah." I scanned my eyes over the certificate again and saw that a Demetrius Cleveland had been the informant, the one to report the death. I spun the computer to face Santiago and pointed. "Well, that's interesting isn't it?" I said.

"Very," Santiago said as he wrote in his notebook. "Looks like I'll need to have a conversation with Mr. Cleveland."

"He must have his dad's name," I said, sure that Santiago had thought of the same thing.

"Or his grandfather's. We're talking almost a hundred years ago, so it could even be his great-grandfather."

"True," I said. "Let me build out Earnestine's family tree, and then I'll dig into the Clevelands, okay?"

"Sounds good," Santiago said as he went back to the email he was composing to Deputy Winslow. He'd told me he wanted her fully informed when she began her shift in a few hours.

As I went back into the genealogy files, I was able to build a family tree fairly quickly for Earnestine going back a couple of generations. It also appeared she had children, a boy and a girl, who had children of their own. Earnestine's grandchildren were still alive, but because of privacy laws, which I totally understood and respected, I couldn't find out who they were in this way.

Instead, I took another tack and reached out to three people who had built family trees that included Earnestine and Fountain Greene and asked if they could give me any more information about them since I was doing research on the church history. I didn't really like that I wasn't telling them the whole story, but I knew it was too soon to tell anyone about our suspicions that Earnestine had been killed.

Now, it was time for me to see what I could find out about the Cleveland family. I expected I could simply call Mary and ask her, but I didn't want to cast suspicion on Demetrius's ancestors unnecessarily. It would be better to see what I could uncover on my own and then let Santiago take over.

Within a few minutes, I had Demetrius's family line traced back into the 1890s, and each of the first-born sons in a particular line was named Demetrius, after his father. The Demetrius Cleveland that I had met today was the fifth. But it looked like his great-grandfather was alive and an adult in 1928. Which meant he was probably strong enough to push a middle-aged woman down a flight of stairs.

I told Santiago what I'd found, and he groaned quietly. "I really like that guy," he said.

"Me, too."

He sighed. "He gave me his number. I'll call him shortly."

The sound of car tires on the driveway brought me to my feet, and I quickly cleared our pizza plates from the table as Santiago moved the computers out of toddler reach just in time because an intense knock on the door announced my son's return to our home.

"Who is it?" I said

"It's Sawyer Lee Sutton," a small voice said.

"Are you selling something?" I asked as I cracked the door.

"Mama, it's me. Let me in," the tiny blonde child said with a grin.

"Oh, it's you. Well, then, yes, come in." I rubbed his head as he hugged my legs and then watched as he launched himself into Santiago's arms.

"Look, Daddy," Sawyer said as he turned to look at his dad in the doorway. "Santi's here."

"So he is," my ex, Davis, said with a little disgust. He knew Santiago and I were dating, knew and had approved that he spend time with our son. But I imagined it was still awkward, not that I was dating, but that Sawyer loved Santiago so much. Still, I knew that no matter how much I assured Davis, Santiago would always feel like a threat because, well, most of the world felt like a threat to Davis.

"Buddy," I said as Santiago slid Sawyer to the floor, "Why don't you and I show your dad how you can do the monkey bars?"

"Okay," my little boy said as he took his dad's hand and led him to the playground.

I smiled at Santiago, who grinned back. "I'll clean up and get the living room ready for movie night."

"Perfect," I said as I kissed his cheek and headed to the playground myself.

Twenty minutes later when Davis left for home and Sawyer was getting the circles under his eyes that said how tired he was, my boy and I climbed the hill back to the house and settled in with popcorn, Sprite, and *Monsters, Inc.* Sawyer insisted on sitting between Santiago and me on the loveseat, which meant he basically sat on each of us halfway, but I don't think any of us minded.

Within fifteen minutes, Sawyer was sound asleep with his watered-down soda in his hand and drool running down Santiago's uniform. It was absolutely adorable, and I snapped a quick picture that I assured my boyfriend would not end up on social media.

Typically, I treasured the small gift of putting my very busy son to bed and watching him sleep for a few minutes, but tonight, when Santiago offered to carry him up and tuck him into my bed, I let him. The two of them seemed so comfortable, and for the first time, I let myself imagine this could be a regular thing.

As Santiago made his way up the stairs, Beauregard quickly moved into his seat on the couch, warm as it was, and pitty-patted the cushion into perfection before curling up. He knew full well that he'd be asked to move, but even five minutes of warmth and cuddling was enough to make the effort worth it.

Soon, though, Santiago was back, and Beau allowed me to unceremoniously dump him to the floor so he could go curl up in the chair or on, heaven forbid, the memory foam bed I splurged on for him.

As Santiago returned to the couch, he placed my cross-stitch basket in front of me and picked up the remote. "Up for more *Long Way Around*?"

I smiled. The documentary with Ewan MacGregor and his best friend on their expedition to ride their motorcycles around the world was one that both Santiago and I enjoyed, although for different reasons. He loved the motorcycles themselves and all things to do with the ride. I loved the various cultures and travel experiences . . . and, well, Ewan MacGregor.

This was one of the things I appreciated about Santiago most, the ability to recognize what Sawyer and I needed and to go along with that. I knew he had a lovely garden at his own house that he might want to tend in these evening daylight hours, and he was always working on some sort of home improvement project.

But since I needed to be in my house or on the porch when Sawyer was sleep, he contented himself with TV and my company when necessary. Other nights, we went for hikes or got dinner in town . . . or gardened at his house or mine, some-thing that was a favorite for both of us. Our relationship was going well, and I was glad for that, even if I was still quite content to take things slow.

After a couple of episodes, a few hundred stitches, and a

lovely goodnight kiss, Santiago headed to his house, and I got
ready for bed. Beau decided he would take to his own bed for
the night, so I climbed the stairs and slid into the cool sheets
beside my sleeping son. I was out in seconds.

5

The next morning, both of us slept in until almost eight, and I think we needed it because neither of us moved quickly to get out from under the covers that Beau had decided he needed to hold down sometime in the middle of the night.

When we did get up, though, Sawyer was ready to go and didn't even request his usual chocolate milk and videos on the couch. Instead, he wanted to head outside, take his bathroom break (country boys!), and play with his toy lawnmower. I, however, was not as quick moving and headed straight for the kettle and French press. Coffee was most definitely in order.

I had a lot of legwork to do for both my real job and the even more pressing research into the death of Earnestine Greene and the Monacan burial ground, and while Sawyer was getting more and more able to entertain himself, I didn't think working in ten-minute spurts was going to be enough today. So I called my step-mom, Lucille, and asked if she and Dad were up for some time with a three-year-old today.

"Of course," she said. "Would you mind if we took him for a

drive? Your dad wants to get some flowers for the garden, and I know this garden center that has a playground and ice cream."

"That sounds perfect." I felt a pang of regret that I couldn't go along because plants, ice cream, and my son on a playground were three of my favorite things, but I was grateful for the time to write. "Want me to bring him by?"

"That would be great. See you in an hour or so?"

"Awesome. Thank you."

"Thank you for letting us spend time with our grandson." She hung up, and I went into "get ready" mode, which included asking Sawyer to put on clothes about twelve times until he actually did.

An hour later, my son dressed by himself, our bellies full of cream of wheat with almonds and raisins, and the full bug collecting kit in his fox backpack, and we were off. Sometimes just getting out the door felt like it took all my energy for the day, but I knew that once I got settled into Mika's comfy chairs with my laptop, I'd rally . . . and Sawyer would race through the day without pause, in all likelihood. I was going to miss him, but sometimes, the quiet was worth that ache.

Once Sawyer was settled in with his grandparents, I headed downtown to Mika's store, my second office. I liked working around other people, and when I worked here, I sometimes got to take breaks and help Mika with customers or restocking. Plus, I got to see my best friend and drink the coffee she kept for customers.

Mondays were usually slow in the store because the small stream of tourist traffic that came through on their way up to the nearby Blue Ridge Parkway usually dwindled after the weekend. So Mika used Mondays to do her paperwork and orders.

For the first bit of time I was there, we sat with our laptops and diligently did our work. I was trying to dig a bit more deeply into Earnestine Greene's life by looking for old newspaper articles about her, her husband, and the church, and from the sighs of frustration from Mika's chair, I gathered she was trying to order the high end stock she was known for on the budget that didn't really afford such things.

Eventually, when her sighs turned into groans, I saved my work, closed the laptop, and got up to get us both coffee. When I handed her the mug that said, "Save Me From Mondays," she smiled, closed her own computer, and said, "I hate money."

"Me, too," I said. Both of us were entrepreneurs at heart, and we knew the challenges of running our own businesses. But as women in our middle lives, we were weary of the constant struggle to make ends meet. We'd been tying together those ends for decades now, and more than anything, we simply wanted enough to lift the constant undercurrent of worry. "Is business getting any better? More steady?" I asked.

Mika took a long sip of her coffee. "It is, but now, I need to make some big investments to get to the place where it's just not covering expenses."

"Like a website?" I said. Mika had a very basic website that she built herself, and she could take orders through it. But the system was clunky and didn't include all her inventory. She needed to hire a designer to build a real online store for her, but that cost was beyond her means, even though she'd been saving for it since she opened.

"Right. I think I could get lots of web orders if I just had the right site with an easy process for ordering." She sighed again. "But . . ."

"But that costs a lot of money." I knew the feeling. I used mostly auction sites to sell my wares, and while I had a basic webpage to tell about my business if someone searched for me online, it wasn't anything like what I could have. "Maybe we can brainstorm a way to bring in some extra cash together? Let's think about that, okay?"

Mika nodded. "Okay. But tell me what you're finding." I'd

caught her up on what we'd learned the day before and how
Santiago didn't think it likely that Earnestine had just
randomly fallen down her own stairs on that particular day.
"Not much. The church did the normal church things –
dinners, funerals, weddings, homecomings – and Earnestine
seemed like she played her part as pastor's wife really well. She
was at all the events, and all the articles in the local paper were
flattering about her attentiveness to her husband and her
parishioners.

"I keep thinking about those journals, though," I told Mika.
"She never complained about the church or baking casseroles
every day, of course. But there was something about her tone
…"

"Yeah, I know what you mean. She wanted more, I think,
more to fill her time. There's kind of a longing in what she said,
the way she talked about wanting to see Morocco in that one
journal." Mika's eyes grew wistful. She had always wanted to
travel more, but owning a business meant she didn't get much
time off.

"Exactly," I said. I sat and drank my coffee for a few
moments as I thought about how most of the women I knew,
mothers, business owners, caregivers for aging parents, longed
to travel or just "get out more" and how most of us gave up that
ability to live other dreams. I wondered how many of the men I
knew had to sacrifice the same way. "Anyway, it seems like
something must have made her feel the need to tell what she
knew on that particular day, right?"

Mika nodded.

"But I can't figure out what. I think I need to dig into the
church records more," I said.

"Mary can help you out with that, right?" Mika asked.

"I think so. And hopefully, we can also piece together how
the church came to be built on a burial ground." I'd done
enough work around old places to know that cemeteries got

lost to history sometimes, but the Monacans buried their dead in raised mounds. It seemed unlikely that no one at least recognized the oddity of the land in that spot, but then again, farmers moved neatly laid out gravestones that were in their way when plowing to this day. We see what we want to see, I guess. "I think I need to go to the clerk's office and dig into the land records a little."

Mika stood up. "And I need to create a new window display of some big chunky yarn to help people start thinking about their fall projects. It's ninety degrees today, but soon we'll be into sweater weather." She smiled, and I was glad to see her mood had lifted a little.

I packed up my bag and told my best friend I'd be back to help her accessorize the new window display in a couple of hours. I had some fun trinkets in my storage space at Saul's yard, and I thought I'd pick them up and bring them over for her to use after I made some headway in the research.

Fortunately, the county office building, where the public records for Octonia were stored, was just up the street from Mika's shop. So even walking in the sauna that was a Virginia August didn't get me too sweaty, or well, no sweatier than anyone else in this heat. I did groan with delight when the blast of air conditioning hit me as I walked into the courthouse and I made my way through the metal detector before swinging a right away from the courtrooms to the clerk's office.

It had been years since I spent time in libraries, but this room was pretty close. The walls were lined with huge bookshelves, and the scent of old paper filled the air. Everyone working here – mostly people researching property titles for real estate agents and banks – was quiet and focused, and the only sound was the flip of pages or the clatter of computer keyboards. I loved it here.

But this bit of work today was going to be cumbersome, and not just because I was about to get an arm workout by lugging deed books around. I had to pare my way back through history to find when the church acquired its land and from whom. So I started with the computer and looked up the church name to find the Plat Number. It was always surprising to most people that who owned what land was public record, but anyone anywhere could find who owned what property and get their address too. Some folks felt like that was a violation of privacy.

For researchers like me, though, it was amazing, and I was soon zipping back through property records and deed transfers. I knew that the church had been founded in 1908, so I scanned to find the church name in the deed index and then pulled the 1907-1911 deed book from the shelf.

There, in the Clerk of Courts elegant hand-writing, I read about how a man named Elijah Morris had sold the land to the church for the price of one dollar. Essentially, he'd gifted the land to the church, but in order for the church to avoid paying taxes, he charged them for it. I looked quickly at the sketch of the plat and noticed right away that the church now owned what was two plats back in 1908.

Following a hunch, I looked back at the deed index and saw that in 1928, the church had also made a purchase, and when I looked at the date on the actual deed, it was dated August 8, 1928, the exact day that Earnestine Greene had decided to tell the church leadership about the burial ground. The exact day she had died.

The church had again bought the land for one dollar, this plot from a man named Nicholas Benfer. I knew Benfer's name, but only because it was the street name for a road just outside town, a couple of blocks up from the church itself. That wasn't a coincidence. It couldn't be.

I texted Santiago immediately and asked him to join me when he could. "Be there in fifteen," he replied. The perks of being a small town sheriff often included easy availability. Although I didn't know if that was always a perk, especially when people expected him to be available at all hours. I hoped I wasn't burdening him with this, but I didn't think I was.

While I waited for him, I decided to follow the trail of paper back from Elijah Morris and Nicholas Benfer, and by the time Santiago arrived and received a dispensation from the women at the front desk to bring me a coffee if we promised to sit away from the books, I had tied both pieces of land to a plantation named BelAirre and once owned by Benfer's ancestor, also a Nicholas Benfer.

Santiago and I slid into the back room of the research area and spread out with our coffee and my notes, leaving all the irreplaceable books on the reading stands out front. I showed him what I'd found and then explained what it meant. "All of that land was once part of Benfer's plantation. I have to keep digging, but I expect we're going to find two things – that Benfer sold a lot of pieces of his property in the years after the Civil War and that, maybe, Elijah Morris was connected to BelAirre somehow."

"Connected?" Santiago asked.

"It's likely that he was either a business associate of Benfer or, just maybe, he was enslaved by Benfer. It wasn't uncommon for former enslavers to gift or sell land to the people they enslaved because it meant those people would stay close and keep working for them."

Santiago studied the page of notes in front of him and then looked up at me. "You know the Benfers?"

I shook my head. "Benfer Road, yes, but I didn't know the family was still around."

"Yeah. Still around. Good folks. They live in that big white house on Benfer Road. You know it, I bet – huge black walnuts around it, set off with the mountains in the background," he said.

I did know the house because I ogled it every time I drove by. It was gorgeous, and the setting was perfect. It showed off the house but still gave the occupants privacy. I'd often wondered if it had been the big house on a plantation, and it seemed so. "Do you know them well enough for us to visit?" I asked, hope making my voice a little high.

"Yep. They've offered to show me around before, but I hadn't ever taken them up on it. Clearly, I need to give them a call." He smiled at me and reached over and squeezed my hand. "I love how excited you get about historic places, Paisley."

I blushed because of the softness of his words and the weight behind them. He got me, and everything about that made me heart race. "Thanks. Thanks for knowing how much I love this stuff."

He smiled. "I'll go out and call them right now. Are you okay telling them what you're researching? Leaving out the burial ground and murder part, of course."

"Absolutely. I don't like asking for things without having something to give, so you can tell them that I'll work up the full history of this land we're researching and share it with them if you want." I was careful not to say I'd look at the whole planta- tion history because that was a month's long undertaking. But I could trace this chain of custody for these particular plats easily enough, especially since I was almost there.

"Be back in a minute," Santiago said and kissed my hand before taking our empty cups and heading back out.

I followed him back to my workspace and quickly learned that the Benfers had gotten all their land – over five thousand acres – from a land grant in the late 1700s. They sold a number of small parcels of five to ten acres to various people in the 1890s and on into the twentieth century, but it seemed like they still owned a sizable swath of property right around their house.

A quick look at the will index showed that Nicholas Benfer had died in 1932, and when I looked for other Benfers, I found a long line of Nicholas Benfers including the father, grandfather, and back to the first of seven Nicholas's, Nicholas I. The first three Nicholas's had died in 1904, 1888, and 1829, respectively. I pulled out the will book of the Nicholas who died in 1932 first and scanned past the legal jargon to see if anything was left to people outside the family.

Sure enough, six acres was given to Elijah Morris "and his heirs" at Benfer's death. All of the other property passed, per the usual, to Benfer's children, so I knew there was something significant happening with this gift.

Santiago came back and said the Benfers were happy to see us in an hour if we could make it that soon, and the smile that broke across my face must have been enough confirmation because Santiago took out his phone and texted a quick message.

Then, I realized I needed to figure out how Elijah Morris was connected to the Benfers before we went, and I put Santiago to work looking at census records online while I dug back into the will books.

My boyfriend was a quick study on the database and soon had located Elijah Morris in every census available from 1870 on. He had been born, it seemed in about 1825, which made him a contemporary of the father of the Nicholas Benfer who died in 1932. But interestingly enough, he was identified on the 1870 census as black. "So he and Benfer couldn't have been friends," Santiago stated.

I shook my head. "It's more complicated than that. If, as I suspect, Morris was enslaved by Benfer's family, then the men probably grew up together. It wasn't an equal friendship by any means, but that doesn't mean they weren't friends in some sense." I stared at the will where Nicholas gifted Morris land, "especially given this." I tapped the page.

Santiago nodded. "So somehow, maybe, slavery didn't destroy their relationship."

I shrugged. "Maybe. I need to look into that more. Do we have a few more minutes before we have to leave?"

"Sure. We'll put on my lights and siren if need be," he said with a laugh.

I pulled the will index over again and scanned for the Benfer name, jotting down book and page numbers quickly and sending Santiago to pull all three books. Soon, he and I were scanning the wispy handwriting to see if we could find any mention of Elijah or, more magically, the Morris family. Since slaves didn't carry surnames legally, most of them were simply called by first names, but I was hopeful that someone would actually acknowledge the surname they used (because they did use surnames) in a legal document. I'd only seen it once or twice, but those two unicorns of history kept my hopes up.

This time, though, we didn't see the name Morris. But we did find Elijah's name in the will of the first Nicholas's great-grandfather, who died in 1829 and bequeathed his grandson a woman named Anna and her son Elijah, age four. I leaned back and stared at the page. Elijah and Nicholas the Fif5th were the same age, and so they had, indeed, been raised together, likely in part by Elijah's mother since enslaved women were often expected to mind the master's children, too.

Every part of me wanted to see what I could find out about Elijah Morris's descendants so that I could share this information with them if they didn't have it already, but we were out of time . . . and if we didn't rush now, we would need those sirens and lights.

Quickly, we put all the books back, said a rushed thank you to the helpful women up front, and sprinted to Santiago's car. We would have made it right on time even without, but Santiago spun his lights into action and whizzed us down the road fast enough to make me grin.

As we pulled up to the white house with two-story wooden

columns, I suddenly felt nervous. A lot of plantation owners in this area resented the history of their family, even if they still lived off the wealth. I'd had some really good conversations with people who had bought old plantations, but the "old money," so to speak, wasn't usually as amenable to these chats. I hoped that their quick invitation indicated that the Benfers were interested, at least, if not actually willing to be helpful.

A beautiful woman with long brown hair tied back with a scarf greeted us. She looked to be just a bit older than me, and she wasn't all done up, no make-up on her pink cheeks as best I can tell. "Mrs. Benfer, it's nice to see you," Santiago said.

"*Sheriff* Shifflett, how many times have I asked you to call me Veronica?" She smiled as her blue eyes flashed. "You must be Paisley? I've been following your newsletter for some time. So nice to meet you."

I felt a blush wash over my face. "You read what I write?"

"Every week," she said. "I'm an amateur history buff. Comes with marrying into this beautiful old place, I suppose." She waved her hand and gestured for us to precede her through the front door.

The entry hall was gorgeous. A wooden staircase with a stunning mahogany railing led up to the second floor and a hallway moved behind it to what, it seemed, might have been an addition onto the original house. The floors were wide pine and it looked like the original wainscotting and original decorative crown molding against the plaster ceiling. It was understated and beautiful, and I told her so.

"Well, that's a high compliment coming from someone with your knowledge, Paisley. Would you like a tour?" she asked with a smile.

I resisted the urge to jump up and down and put my hands in the air and instead responded with a simple, "Yes," before following her through the door to the right and into a lovely dining room set with a round table. As we moved through the rooms, I noticed the thin slits in the ceilings for the HVAC system to do its work. The bathrooms that had been added over the years were spacious but tucked away so as not to disrupt the original layout of the house overly much. It was a gorgeous home, historical and comfortable.

"I've seen a lot of houses of this period, and yours is, by far, the most homey," I said as she led us into a light-filled kitchen addition on the back of the house beyond a formal library. "It feels like people live here."

Veronica smiled. "That's good, because we do," she said. "It's our home, and we want people who visit to feel welcome."

I smiled and decided to make myself comfortable in one of the padded seats at the rustic farm table. I pulled out my notes and took a minute, as Veronica prepared iced tea, to gather my thoughts into a cogent pattern that would make sense to someone other than me.

Given her congeniality, I decided to get the hard stuff out of the way and begin by talking about Nicholas Benfer and Elijah Morris. I asked her how much she knew about her husband's family, and she grinned. "You mean the long time of Nicholases?" she asked.

"Well, yes," I said. "Is your husband a Nicholas, too?"

"Nick, but yes. He's the eighth. Talk about a bear for genealogy work."

I laughed. "Yep, I'm always telling people they should name their children things like *popsicle* so that historians can differentiate them later in life."

Santiago laughed. "Your children aren't named potato and peach pie, are they?"

"Nope, but I did end the line of Nicholas. We have a Diane and a Milo." She smiled and gestured toward a picture of two young adults on a window sill nearby. "They're both off at college, and I miss them terribly." She sighed and looked back at me. "But while I know the Nicholases, I don't know much more. None of us do, I'm afraid. Too busy with work and kids to dig in, I guess."

I nodded. It was a familiar refrain. Most people cared about their family, but the people they knew or had known, not generations back. It was hard to carry around the stories of people we did know much less the generations of stories behind us. "I get it. Someday I'm going to get around to researching more of my own family stories," I said with a smile.

I cleared my throat. "And I expect you know that your husband's family got this land as part of a land grant and that then," I paused and took a breath, "they built their wealth through slavery."

She nodded without hesitation. "We don't pretend that's not the base of what we have here, the base of everything really. But we don't know much. I'd like to know more, though, much more." She put her hand over mine. "Can you tell me more?"

I swallowed and smiled. "I can tell you a bit, and if you want, I can help you find out more about that part of your family's history."

"Oh, that would be amazing. I'd like to hire you, if I could." She studied my face. "I hope that's not offensive. I just like to pay people for their work."

"Not offensive at all. I'm in the midst of something right now, but how about we set a date to talk more about that in a couple of weeks?" My heart was dancing. I had been hoping to land some work in research to complement my salvaging projects, and here was my first opportunity, and a big one at that.

"Great," she said with a huge smile. "Now, what did you want to talk about today?"

I handed her a sheet of paper where I'd jotted down the information about Nicholas the Original and Elijah and explained what it meant. Then I told her I was researching the history of Bethel Church and that both Elijah and Nicholas the

Fifth had basically gifted land to the congregation over a twenty-year period. "I know it's a long shot, but do you know anything about a friendship between Nicholas and Elijah?"

She shook her head. "This is literally the first time I've heard Elijah Morris's name." She stared at the piece of paper in her hand, "But do you have a minute? I do have something that might help."

I nodded, and she hurried off into the library.

"That's exciting, Pais," Santiago said. "A research gig."

I laughed. "It is, and for one of the biggest landholding plantations in Octonia. Exciting."

Veronica came back in the room and handed me a framed photograph. In it, two boys – one white and one black – had their arms around each other as they held fishing poles by what looked like it might be the Fleur River. "Whoa," I said as I studied the image.

I didn't know much about historical clothing, but it looked like the black boy was wearing a pair of short breeches made from some sort of rough cloth. And the white boy had on suspenders and a shirt that looked much finer than his friend's. I would definitely have to research the date of the photo more, but my heart was racing with possibility.

"Do you have any idea who these boys are?" I asked Veronica as I passed the photo to Santiago.

She shook her head. "It's been hanging on the wall in the living room as far back as Nick can remember. And when you mentioned Nicholas and Elijah . . ."

"Right," I said. "Do you mind if I take a picture of it?"

"Just take the photograph itself. You might need it for research, and photos of photos get all grainy." She smiled, and I found myself liking this woman more and more. I was eager to get working on her project, but I needed to find out what I could about the church and the burial ground first.

"Thanks so much. I'll let you know what I find out, okay?"

She smiled. "I'd love that." She turned to Santiago. "Do you mind if I ask you a question that you can simply not answer if you prefer?"

"Sure," he said.

"The police tape at Bethel – does that have anything to do with all of this?" She looked sincere and interested, and I was curious what Santiago would tell her.

"In a way, yes," he said. "You'll read about it in tomorrow's paper, I think," he said with a glance at me. "Chief Stephenson is releasing a statement later today," he said.

I nodded and found I was glad. It was always easier to work when everything was out in the open, and I didn't have to withhold information from the people I needed to talk to.

"We believe there may be a Monacan burial ground under the church," he said. "In her research, Paisley found some records that indicate that, and the chief of the Monacan nation has confirmed that's a very strong possibility." He said everything in his efficient sheriff's voice, but I could see the emotion in his tight jaw. "We're beginning a formal investigation into that possibility."

Veronica looked down at the table. "And my husband's family gave the land for the church." She looked over at me. "So they donated a burial ground?"

I sighed. "Technically, yes, but maybe they didn't know."

Veronica stood and began to pace around the kitchen. "How could they not know something like that?"

I wanted to explain to her that cemeteries and graveyards were lost to history all the time, but I didn't think that would be a comfort to this compassionate, open woman. "I don't know," I said instead.

She turned to Santiago. "Would you be willing to introduce me to the chief? I'd like to see how we might help make reparations for this."

I held in my gasp. In all the years I'd been researching

history and the way one group of people had hurt other people, I had never once heard someone who was benefitting from the harm outright offer to repair it. Usually that step only came with years of work and effort. I felt tears well up in my eyes.

"I will call her right now, if that's okay," Santiago said.'

Veronica nodded, and while Santiago dialed, I asked if I might walk around outside. I wanted to give them privacy for this conversation, and I also needed a minute to myself to gather my emotions.

"Make yourself at home," she said.

I smiled and headed out the back door to look out from the small rise that gave the house a gorgeous view of the Blue Ridge beyond. I could easily see the barn down below closer to the pasture and what looked like a smoke house and maybe a kitchen just a few steps away. Down the hill toward the other side, two standing chimneys faced each other like sentinels, and I knew immediately that was probably a slave quarter for the house servants. I took out my notebook and made a few notes before snapping a couple of pictures.

Then, I walked around to the front of the building and looked out over the rolling hills toward town. There, just beyond the next small rise, I could see the church's white steeple. Between the church building itself, the manse looked like a small cottage, but it was very clear, from this angle, that it sat at a slightly higher elevation than the church itself.

It was possible that Nicholas the Fifth hadn't known about the burial ground, but from this angle, it certainly didn't seem likely.

6

O n the ride back downtown, Santiago gave me the details about Veronica's call with Chief Stephenson, after getting their permission to share. They'd both wanted me to know so that when I wrote about the story, I could share what they'd agreed.

Veronica had offered to pay for all archaeological work and any work of remembrance, as they'd put it, that the Monacan Nation might want done. The nation would have full control, but they wouldn't have to pay for a thing.

Both Santiago and I were stunned and so overjoyed at this development, and he said, "Chief Stephenson was very glad, too. They don't have a lot of money, but they were going to figure out how to make this happen."

"I know Saul was going to donate all his work," I said, "but archaeologists can't work for free any more than I can."

"Right, and Veronica realized that and assured the Chief that she and her husband were only going to be the silent bene- factors without any expectations." He glanced over at me. "They do want to be anonymous though."

"Absolutely," I said. "I won't say anything to anyone, and I certainly won't write about that."

Santiago smiled. "Thanks. Now, what's your next step?"

"Well, I need to make a call to a friend who studies historical clothing and see if I can put a date on this photo." I held the image in my lap and ran my finger over the curling flowers on the silver frame. With a spur of inspiration and confidence in Veronica's trust, I flipped the frame over, bent back the thin nails that were holding a small board in place, and stared at the words written on the back of the image.

"Nicholas and Eli, Age 8"

I sucked in a quick breath, and Santiago looked over at me. "You okay?"

I nodded as he pulled into the parking space in front of Mika's car. "I am. Just look." I showed him the back of the photo, and he smiled.

"Well, look at that," he said. "You were right."

"I was . . . and it looks like I may need to start on the Benfer's research sooner rather than later." I had to dig a lot into their family story, and if I was going to do that, I might as well keep track of everything, not just a few things. "I'll call her later."

"Sounds good. I'm talking to Demetrius this afternoon, too. I don't know what, if anything, I'll be able to tell you about Earnestine's death, but I wanted you to know I'm looking into it." He stepped out and came around to open my car door while I put the picture frame back together. Then, he gave me a quick kiss and headed back to his office up the street.

I went right into Mika's shop, texted Lucille to be sure everything was going fine with them, and when assured that I had at least another two hours, I dove in. I went through every public record I could online to see what I could find about Elijah Morris and Nicholas Benfer I. Soon, I had basic life stories – birthdays, marriages, children, employment – for both of them.

Nicholas had been a "farmer," as the nomenclature of slavery-designated plantation owners, and in the first years after Emancipation, Elijah was listed as a blacksmith, a fact that meant he had probably worked in that role on BelAirre in the years he was enslaved. Both men stayed in their professions throughout their lives, which wasn't really surprising. Neither was the fact that they lived near to, maybe even next to, each other throughout their lives. On the census, they are always listed within two to three houses of one another, and I took this to indicate that they might have, indeed, remained at least friendly. Or if not friendly, then at least connected through proximity and maybe employment.

But nothing in the online public record explained why Nicholas had willed that six acres to Elijah. That was the rich information, the information that was too personal to warrant a place in public history. That was what I would need to find in the Benfer's records, if they had them.

I took Veronica Benfer's card out of my back pocket and dialed her number. She answered on the second ring, her voice light and fun. "Veronica, it's Paisley. Any chance you might be available for coffee tomorrow morning?"

"Oh, I'd love that. You found something already?" I could hear the excitement in her voice.

"I did . . . but I'm also wondering if we could start work on the research you wanted right away. I'm thinking it might be useful to us all." I was nervous, afraid that I was pushing too hard with this woman I just met.

"That would be amazing," she said. "I talked with Nick after you left, and he's excited, too. Mind if I see if he's free to join us in the morning?"

"Perfect." I asked if she knew the coffee shop downtown, and she assured me that she did.

I did a little dance of excitement and then turned to ask Mika if she minded having Sawyer with her in the morning. In a few weeks Sawyer was going to start morning preschool, and my schedule would open up a lot more. But until then I needed help, and of course Mika was happy to give it. She had a range of activities for Sawyer at the store, and I expected I'd have a collection of God's Eyes made from scraps of yarn and popsicle sticks to decorate a window with. I loved that idea.

When Sawyer got home that night, we spent a couple of hours watching videos of thunder storms and tornadoes, his latest YouTube obsession, and playing with his bubble machine. Beauregard loved the bubbles for approximately three minutes, and then he found them profoundly annoying. His annoyance was Sawyer's delight because it made Beau leap and bat at the bubbles as they drifted across the yard.

When it was time to wind down for bed, both Sawyer and Beau were exhausted and I was content from a good evening with my son. We did a bath and climbed into bed to read, and before I finished *Can I Give You A Squish?*, Sawyer was sound asleep with his head on my leg.

I intended to do more research on the Benfer family before calling it quits for the night. But the fatigue hit while I made my tea, so I opted to catch up on *Doctor Who* while I worked on the tires for Sawyer's cross-stitch bulldozer. A few dozen stitches and an episode in, I called it quits myself and went up to bed.

FORTUNATELY, my brain didn't quit, and when I woke up, I had a clear agenda for my conversation with the Benfers and even more excitement about the project, both for them and to see how what we'd already learned about their family tied into the situation at Bethel Church.

As Sawyer watched his morning Blippi videos, I called Mary to let her know my plans for the morning and to let her know what I'd found out about the history of her church. She was super excited to learn about Elijah Morris and offered to meet up with me at Mika's store later to talk about what she knew and how it might help.

"I think you'll be excited, Pais," she said just before she hung up, and I did a little wiggle because it seemed like, maybe, we were going to make some headway. Sawyer sat down with his videos and actually began to eat his grapes and cheese slices, so I took the moment to let Santiago know my plans via text.

He called almost immediately. "That's great news," he said. "I'm supervising demolition over at the house today. Well, Saul is supervising. I'm there to 'keep the peace.'" I could hear the smile in his voice.

"You don't think there will be trouble do you?" My excitement had suddenly turned into fear. "No one will make trouble, right?"

"I doubt it, but Chief Stephenson asked me to be on hand. So Savannah and I will hang out, play cards, and hope that I get enough time to kick her tail in gin rummy again." He was trying to ease my fear, and I appreciated the effort.

"Okay, good. If I get a minute, I'll stop by if that's okay." I didn't want to intrude, but given how involved I was in all of this, I really did want to be involved in every part of it.

"Please do. I expect it won't be much to see." He laughed then. "But of course, you know that. This is your job."

I laughed, too. "It's actually pretty fun to watch demo."

"Demo?" Sawyer said from across the table. "Is there big equipment working?"

I smiled at my son.

"When do you start?"

"I'm on my way there now."

"You may have visitors in a couple of minutes. A certain small boy is wanting to see the equipment work." I smiled as Sawyer jumped up with half a slice of cheese in his mouth and ran into the living room. He came back with his hard hat and hammer. "I'm ready."

"See you in a few," Santiago said.

Most of the time, my son is a typical young child who dawdles and stalls when it's time to transition to something new. Today, though, he was out the door and into his seat before I even had a chance to pour him a cup of water for the road. Big equipment for the win.

On the ride over, Saw told me stories about how he and his imaginary sister drove bulldozers and crashed them into buildings while their baby jumped off the roof. His stories tended toward violence and danger quite often, and I was glad for the parenting books that had told me this was common at his age.

I tried to keep my attention on his tales as I drove, but my mind kept leaping ahead to the Benfer research. I couldn't help but wonder what other treasures were tucked away in their house. That photo alone was priceless given how rare photos of enslaved people are, but I had high hopes that maybe they also had boxes of papers in an attic or storage room somewhere.

All my attention came back to the present moment, though, when we got the church. A small gathering of people was sitting with Chief Stephenson in camp chairs under the black walnut trees at the edge of the parking lot, and I could see Demetrius Cleveland and Mary talking near them. Santiago's cruiser was parked right at the entrance to the lot, and when we drove in, he stepped out with Deputy Savannah Winslow beside him.

Sawyer barreled into his legs and hugged him. But his attention was soon diverted as the flatbeds with Saul's equipment pulled up on the street and began to unload. Sawyer put his hardhat on and ran to his Uncle Saul, who scooped him up, took him into the cab of the bulldozer, and let him help unload it.

"Looks like I may have lost him," Santiago said with a smile.

"Nah, he'll come back when he gets tired . . . or when Saul kicks him out," I said as I hugged the sheriff and the deputy, too.

"I was going to suggest he could stay with us, if you wanted," Savannah said. "We can keep an eye on him, and that way, he can be around the big equipment."

"That is if you don't think Mika will mind," Santiago added.

I shook my head. "I don't think she'll mind at all, but just let me check." I texted Mika.

She replied immediately. "Actually, that's better. I have some big news. Stop by?"

I glanced at the time on my phone and saw I had about an hour before meeting the Benfers across the street from Mika's. "She's fine with it, if you're sure you don't mind."

We all looked over to where Sawyer was steering the bulldozer into place in front of the house, a look of sheer delight animating his face. "How could we mind watching true joy in action?" Santiago said.

I kissed him on the cheek and headed over to greet Mary, Demetrius, and Chief Stephenson. Everyone seemed to be a mix of excited and sad, and given that this was exactly how I felt every time I looked at this land now, I understood.

"Are you ready?" I asked the chief and the rest of the members of the tribal council with her. "I know this will be hard."

A man about my age with hair that touched the collar of his blue button-up shirt said, "It will, but it will also be good, renewing." He smiled at me, and I held onto his word – "renewing."

"Good. My son is the enthusiastic bulldozer operator, but don't worry, his Uncle Saul won't let him be disrespectful," I said with a sudden flash of worry that my son's delight might be interpreted as frivolity on my part or his. "I've explained to him what's happening here today, and I think he understands."

Chief Stephenson stood. "Play is a form of joy, and joy is never disrespectful," she said. "Can I meet your son?"

"I'd love to introduce you." We walked over to where Sawyer sat on the disabled bulldozer moving levers and making sounds while Saul instructed his crew on their process for the day. "Sawyer, I want you to meet someone. Can you come down?"

"How about I come up? Would that be okay?" Chief Stephenson said.

Sawyer looked at me, and I nodded. "Okay," he said quietly.

"I'm Beth," she said. "You are here to help me honor my ancestors. Your mom told you about that, right?"

Sawyer nodded. "Your grandparents are buried here like my grandma is buried in a graveyard in town." He had been listening.

"That's right, and as the chief of our people, it's part of my job to be sure these people are taken care of." She slid into the seat next to him as he made room for her to join him.

"You're a real Indian chief?" he said with awe, and I wanted to correct him, remind him that we said *Native American,,* but I didn't have the chance.

"That's right. I'm Chief Stephenson, chief of the Monacan Indian Nation. Thank you for coming to help us today," she said.

"You're welcome," Sawyer replied. "Let me show you how this works."

Chief Stephenson looked over at me and winked, and I smiled back as I felt Santiago come up and take my hand.

"We've got him, Paisley," he said. "Have fun researching." He kissed me lightly and turned to Sawyer. "Can I learn, too?"

"Sure," Sawyer said as he glanced at me, and I waved goodbye and explained that he was staying here for the morning. "Yay," he said and then went back to teaching our friends how the bulldozer worked.

I waved to Saul and then spoke briefly to Mary and Demetrius before heading further into town to see Mika. I was very curious about what the big news was, but I hoped it wouldn't take too long. I didn't want to be late for my first paying research clients.

As soon as I walked in the door, Mika said, "I know how we can make money for our websites," she said.

I took a deep breath, put my hands on her shoulders, and said, "Okay, how?" My mind was already a little full with all the things, but her excitement was almost as contagious as Sawyer's.

"A pop-up shop at the Charlottesville Farmers' Market for a few weekends." She smiled at me with a smug satisfaction that lit up her eyes.

"A pop-up shop, like the ones on all those reality shows? Are we that cool?" I asked.

"We are not that cool, but we can pretend to be." She went on to explain what we could sell – yarn, obviously, but also Dad's picture frames, small but intriguing pieces of architectural salvage, and the knitted items that she had made for display around the shop. "It won't cost us anything more than the rent for the space, and I think we could make a few hundred dollars each weekend."

I nodded and found myself feeling hopeful about the idea, even though it was going to be more work for two people who already had more than enough to do. "It does sound doable," I said. "And maybe we could put out sign-up sheets for our newsletters and make some brochures to advertise our businesses."

"Exactly," Mika said with a little hop. "So you'll do it?"

I sighed. "I'll do it."

"Great," she said, "because I booked us a spot for Saturday." She batted her eyelashes and kissed my cheek. "Now off with you to do your *other*, other job."

I rolled my eyes and grinned. "You owe me wine, you know?"

"Oh yes, definitely," she said and waved as I headed across the street to my meeting.

I had a lot going on these days, but all of it was so exciting. As a friend had once told me, I have the capacity to do a lot of things, but once that capacity is reached, I burn out quickly. So as I smiled at the Benfers in the coffee window, I reminded myself to give myself the timeline I needed to manage all I had going on. I didn't think they'd pressure me, but I could put a lot of pressure on myself if I wasn't mindful.

When I sat down with my vanilla latte and chocolate croissant, Nick Benfer picked up his own chocolate chip scone so we could toast. "Good taste," he said as we "clinked" pastries. Veronica smiled and sipped her drink.

"Thanks for meeting with me so soon. It turns out that if you want to hire me, I'd love to get started as soon as possible. Some of the research I've been doing on Bethel Church has tied into your family, and so I'm eager to see if we can find out more."

"I've told Nick what you shared yesterday, and we plan on going by the church to meet Chief Stephenson after we talk. Do you mind if we share that we are working with you?" Veronica asked.

"Not at all, but I will warn you, when I left there this morning, my son was teaching her how to use a bulldozer. She may be occupied," I said with a laugh.

"Noted," Nick said. "We won't interrupt." He grinned and then said, "So we want to hire you. I want to be clear. Your price. Your timeline. But Veronica is so enamored with your work and your care about the people you research that we are eager to get started, too."

I blushed. "Wow, well then, okay. Thank you." I smiled at Veronica. "Let's talk about what you want to find out."

In unison, they said, "Everything" and then looked at each other.

My eyes went wide. "Everything? Okay. Well, that's something. Everything about what? Your family? The people your ancestors enslaved? The property?"

"Yes," Nick said. "But mostly we want to find out about the people we enslaved." He glanced at his wife. "We want to have them to the farm and ask them in what ways we could honor their ancestors."

I swallowed to keep the tears from spilling. This was exactly the kind of response I had hoped for, the kind of work I hoped to be a part of. "That sounds amazing. Well, one place to start is for you to meet the members of Bethel Church. I expect you know some of them, and I think it's very likely, given what I've already found, that they have ties to your land."

I explained what I'd learned about the photo, which I returned to them as I spoke, and about Elijah Morris and the land for the church. They got so excited, and soon, we were talking about the boxes of papers in their attics (Hallelujah!) and what else I might look into. By the time we'd talked for ninety minutes, I had a clear plan of research, beginning in their attic, and a fee and timeline that not only would help me set up my office at Saul's lot but could jumpstart my website, too.

Our plans set and a generous check for my first month's work in hand, we walked over to the church together. I made introductions and then went to see how Sawyer was doing. He and Savannah were watching one of Saul's crew lift the final section of roof off the building, and my son was enrapt. "Hey Saw," I said, and he waved in my general direction without taking his eyes off the equipment.

"He's having a great time," Savannah said.

"I'm so glad," I said. "No trouble?"

"No trouble of any sort," she said as she tousled Sawyer's

hair. Then, a crease formed between her eyes as she looked toward the entrance of the parking lot.

I followed her gaze and saw a tall, blonde man who looked a little familiar talking with Santiago and Nick Benfer by Santiago's car. Whatever they were saying looked rather unpleasant, and I took Sawyer's hand so that Savannah could go over and see what was up. Not for the first time, I wished I had vampire-like hearing so I'd know what was going on.

But because it was really none of my business and I hadn't been turned into a vampire, I went back to watching Saul's crew take the house down. They were about to bulldoze the walls, and it was going to get very destructive very soon. Sawyer was almost vibrating with anticipation.

Mary came over and joined me, shooting a glance toward the group, which now included Chief Stephenson, standing in the parking lot. "We have got ourselves a mess it seems," she said quietly.

"Really? What's going on?" I asked as I turned away from Sawyer while keeping a tight grip on his hand. The noise of the machinery would block out most of our conversation I hoped.

"Apparently, that's Nick Benfer's brother, and he's claiming to own this land and saying he doesn't want the building taken down," Mary said.

Just then, Saul pushed his bulldozer into the front of the building and collapsed all four walls in one fell swoop.

"Too late," I said as I saw Saul wink at me. That man didn't miss a beat.

Mary grinned. "Oops."

7

H er face grew serious, then. "He doesn't have a claim does he?"

I shook my head. "Not as far as I can tell. The line of title is very clear. He'd have to be able to prove that something illegal happened in order to have any case."

"Okay, good." She looked back toward the group. "You going over there?"

Nick Benfer caught my eye and gave me a little head tilt. "I guess so," I said. "Care to keep me company?"

She studied the group a minute and then said, "Sure, why not?"

Saul was coming out of the bulldozer, so I asked him if Sawyer could "help" him for a few minutes.

The two of us strode toward the group where the tension was so thick it felt like walking through syrup. Well, that could have been the humidity, but it still wasn't a comfortable moment.

As soon as I walked up, Santiago introduced me and Mary to Levi Benfer, and I put out my hand to shake it. He returned the gesture and then turned back to his Santiago. "You need to stop this. I can get a court order if needed."

"That won't be necessary," a woman said behind me, and I turned to see Eliza Dixon from DHR walking toward me. "As the legal authority for cemeteries in the Commonwealth of Virginia, we have already registered this as a potential burial site and are working with the Monacan Nation to confirm the burials here."

"But I have rightful title to this land," Levi said.

"I'm afraid, sir, that we are past the point where that matters. Burial grounds are protected places in Virginia, and given that we are fairly certain human remains lie under this building, we are proceeding." She turned to me. "Sheriff, please let us know if you need anything further." She handed Santiago a stack of papers and then winked at me as she walked toward Chief Stephenson and the rest of the Tribal Council.

Santiago glanced through the papers in his hand. "Looks to be in order. We are proceeding, Mr. Benfer. You are welcome to stay, but I will inform you if, indeed, we do not find burials here. Then, you can take things to court if you'd like."

Levi Benfer glared at Santiago and then turned on his heel and stormed back to his car, kicking up a cloud of gravel dust as he went. He looked just like Sawyer when the three-year-old didn't get his way.

Out of the corner of my eye, I saw Savannah and Santiago give each other a high five, and Nick grinned. "Nick Benfer," he said as he extended his hand to Mary. "Nice to meet you."

Mary introduced herself and then thanked him for his help. "Mind introducing me to your wife?" She looked over to where Veronica sat with Eliza and Chief Stephenson. "I'd like to thank her, too."

"Sure thing," Nick said.

"Mind if I join you?" Savannah asked. Soon, the three of them had joined the circle under the trees

I glanced over to confirm that Sawyer was okay and spotted him next to a tree watching Saul clean up the debris, I turned back to my boyfriend. "Well, that was exciting."

Santiago sighed. "I could do with less excitement, honestly."

I hugged him quickly and then said, "At least we're moving forward, right?"

He nodded.

"What's next? I mean after the building is removed." Saul was making quick work of the debris, and given that two dumpsters had just arrived on the street, it looked like they might have it all cleaned up by the end of the day.

"As soon as we can schedule it, archeologists are coming out. It's not likely given that the church dug a basement, but maybe." He stared as Saul pushed another pile of boards and plaster together.

I thought about that. "That's interesting, right? I mean if they dug down into the ground instead of putting the house on piers like my house, wouldn't they have found bones? Remains of some sort?"

Santiago turned to look at me. "Probably," he said with a grim expression.

I gulped. "So whoever built this house may have known there were people buried here?" My skin crawled with goose bumps. "And they did it anyway?"

He sighed. "I'm afraid that's a firm possibility."

A round of laughter bubbled up from the circle of people nearby. "Do Chief Stephenson and the other Council members know that?"

"They're the ones who suggested it was possible." He took my hand as I sighed again. "But it's also possible that there were no burials in the top layers of earth."

I squeezed his fingers. "So maybe no one's body was disturbed?"

"That's the hope."

At that moment, Sawyer came running over. "Uncle Saul says I can ride with him again. Is that okay, Mama?"

I looked over at Saul, who nodded. "Sure thing, but you do only what Saul says you can." He didn't wait for me to finish and sprinted back as I shouted, "And stay in that seatbelt with Saul."

"Let's go sit down," Santiago said, and we headed toward our friends under the trees and took two of the remaining camp chairs.

Mary said, "Nick and Veronica here were just telling us about the restorations they've been doing down at BelAirre. Did you know they found and preserved the slave cemetery there?"

I smiled. "They just told me this morning. It's amazing, isn't it?"

"It was the least we could do," Veronica said. "And hopefully, Paisley is going to be able to help us find out more about the people buried there."

I blushed. "I hope so. I can't wait to get my hands into those documents."

"You have papers?" Santiago asked.

"Boxes of them, well, trunks really. All in the attic," Nick said.

Chief Stephenson winced. "Are they in good shape? We just found a trove of old documents from a tribe member, but they were all disintegrating from the heat."

"Oh, that's too bad," I said with a groan. "You said these were kept in pretty air-tight trunks, though, right?" I turned back to Veronica.

"Yeah, they're faded a little, but the pages hold together." She looked at Nick. "Once Paisley is done reading them, we want to donate them to the Historical Society."

I had told them that I expected Xzanthia Nicholas, the historical society director, would be eager to get them and that she'd know just how to preserve them well.

"Speaking of which," Nick said, "Why don't we walk over there and introduce ourselves?"

I took that as my cue, too, said my goodbyes, and walked over to near where Saul was still working. "You okay with him staying with you while I go catch Mika up?" I asked when he throttled down the machine low enough to hear me.

"Sure. We're having fun, aren't we, Saw?"

Sawyer nodded and then turned back to the work at hand. As I headed toward the street to walk back to town, Santiago pulled up. "Savannah is staying on site, and I need to go back to the station. Want a lift?"

Given how much I was already sweating without the walk, I didn't hesitate and climbed into the passenger seat of his cruiser. "Thanks," I said.

"You know I always love extra time with you," he said as he took my hand, "but I also just realized I never told you about my conversation with Demetrius yesterday."

"Oh, right? I forgot. What did he say?" Between tracking down Elijah Morris and the demo today and the new job with the Benfers, I had forgotten all about Cleveland family's connection here.

"Honestly, he looked shocked when I told him that his great-great-grandfather had been the one to report Earnestine Greene's death." Santiago put on his signal to pull over across from Mika's store.

"You thought he was telling the truth?" I asked.

"I did, but I don't know that it matters much. Why would that bit of information ever been passed down?"

I nodded. "I guess that's right, unless his ancestor had been the one to kill her." I stared out the window at the traffic going by. "But then, that's probably not the kind of story that would be passed down either."

"He did tell me that his family had been in the church from

the beginning, even back before they had the building and met in a brush arbor," Santiago said.

"I didn't know they were organized that much before the building. Brush arbors were usually used during slavery, when enslaved people wanted to gather for church but didn't have a building. Many of them continued to be used until congregations could gather the means to build an actual church. "Does he have any—?"

"That's why I needed to come back to town," Santiago said as he interrupted me with a smile. "He has some early church records, and he's bringing them to the station in a few minutes."

"Wow. Does Mary know about them?" I asked, worried that my friend, who was the church's official historian, might be left out of the loop.

"She does. There are copies at the church, but Demetrius wanted to keep the originals since they are part of his family history."

"Makes sense," I said. "Do you think he'd let me look at them?"

"Already arranged," Santiago said. "I need to review them first to see if anything relevant to Greene's murder comes up, but if not, Demetrius said I could let you borrow them to see what you can find with your historian's eye."

I kissed him on the cheek and then opened the car door. "I'll come your way whenever you call."

"Sounds good," he said as he put the car in drive. "See you later."

Even with all the hard things – the dishonored graves, the potential murder, the attempted obstruction by Levi Benfer – I was still excited because digging into historical records and finding stories was one of my favorite things. I adored salvaging physical pieces of history, but it was really the stories that I wanted to save most of all.

So I practically bounced into Mika's store at the prospect of having so many great documents to read. "You look chipper," Mika said.

I told her about the morning and about the records from the early history of Bethel Church. "I just have to figure out how to get this work done with Sawyer this week. I don't think I can wait until the weekend to dig in."

Mika grinned. "Well, what if you set up your work station here? You and I can keep an eye on Sawyer together, and Mrs. Stephenson will be in a couple of days this week to help, too."

"You wouldn't mind?" I said.

"Mind?! Are you kidding? I'd love the company, and Sawyer is always so much fun. Besides, I had all my God's Eyes supplies out, and we didn't even get to make a single one." She laughed and pointed toward the back table where I could see a pile of popsicle sticks.

I smiled. "Well, then, that sounds perfect. I'll ask Santiago if he can bring the Cleveland papers here and see if I can go pick up some of the Benfers' things, too." I frowned. "It's going to be a lot of paper, you know?"

"Of course it is. It'll be awesome. And you can get a sense of what it will be like when you have your real office over at Uncle Saul's lot." She moved toward the folding table she used for various projects and picked it up. "I'm setting you up here in the Cozy Nook so that you can spread out."

"But what if someone wants to use it?" I felt bad taking up her quiet corner with my mess.

"Someone does want to use it. You!" She plopped the table down and got a folding chair that she adorned with one of the throw pillows from the upholstered wingbacks nearby. "If someone else wants to sit and knit, they can do that up front. For now, this is your workspace."

I laughed. "You're the best. Lunch is on me for the week."

"Sounds good. I want a falafel." Mika laughed because, of course, the nearest falafel was thirty miles away.

ON THE WAY TO pick up our sandwiches from the local deli at the grocery store for lunch, I stopped by the church to scoop up Sawyer. He was still fascinated by the goings-on, but now he was helping, too. He and Saul were picking up the last pieces of debris around the edges of the basement.

"How does it go from here?" I asked Saul after greeting Sawyer with a quick kiss on the cheek.

"Normally, we'd just get a backhoe and dig out the block, but for obvious reasons, we're not doing that." He smiled as someone walked up behind me, and I turned to see Eliza Dixon joining us. "Ms. Dixon has brought in a team of archaeologists, and we're going to follow their lead for how to take this down, block by block."

"Do you think you'll find any dinosaurs?" Sawyer asked. He and I had watched a show about digging dinosaur bones in Wyoming, and he was very interested in taking part in anything that might give him a huge bone to take home.

"Not likely, Saw, but I'll let you know if I we do," Saul said with a wink. "Deal?"

"Deal," Sawyer said as he rubbed his eyes. That gesture said we were getting close to a melt-down moment, and I needed to get some food into his little body.

"You hungry, Little Man?" I asked.

"Food is yucky," he said, a sure sign he was starving.

"Okay, well, I need to stop and get lunch for Auntie Mika before we go hang out at her store. Will you come help me?" Sawyer was always looking for ways to help.

"Sure," he said, his mood brightening a little. "Let's get her a cupcake."

"Okay, sandwiches, potato chips, and cupcakes it is." I

laughed as he sprinted toward the car. Nothing like the promise of unadulterated sugar to get this boy moving.

The grocery store run went well because I allowed him to pick everything for our lunch. I sure hoped Mika liked ham, cheese, and salami on her sandwich.

Back at her shop, all of us, even Sawyer, dove into our lunches with abandon. The events of the morning had left us all a little wan and weary, and good food with good people was just what we needed.

Given that Sawyer seemed to be still pretty low-key, Mika and I set him up in one of the chairs near my new workspace with a blanket and his videos, and I headed out to get some research materials to bring back.

I hadn't even made it to the Benfers' house when Mika texted to say that Saw was sound asleep. I grinned. He would be good for an hour now, and then, heaven help us, he'd be raring to go when he woke up.

Veronica and Nick met me at the door, and behind them, I saw four archival boxes. My heart skipped a beat with excitement. "You loaded them already? I was all set to dive into decades of dust."

Nick laughed. "It was too embarrassing, and besides, I'm not sure our homeowner's insurance would cover us if you had to be hospitalized for heatstroke up there."

"Fair enough," I said, even though I was a little disappointed I hadn't gotten to see the trunks the papers had been stored in or what other goodies might lurk in that attic. "See anything particularly interesting as you loaded up?"

"We wouldn't know something valuable from a 1904 birthday card, so no," Veronica said.

"Actually that birthday card might be worth something, so I see your point," I grinned. "I'll let you know what I find as I make sense of it, okay?"

"Can't wait," Veronica said as we each hefted a box and

headed to the hatch of my car. I couldn't wait to get started, but first, I needed to make one more stop. Nick went back for the forth box and I said my goodbyes.

Santiago had texted me Demetrius's address, and so I headed back toward town and stopped in front of a lovely brick ranch with a gorgeous rose garden out front. I wasn't much into roses myself, too much work, but when they were well-tended, I loved to walk among them and admire the blooms and scent. Demetrius's flowers were gorgeous, so I took my time as I made my way among them to the front door.

"Those are lovely," I said when he answered the doorbell. "You the gardener?"

He grinned. "I am. It's a tedious hobby, but one I've grown to love. Gives me lots of time to think."

I smiled and took a deep breath to remind myself that no matter what this man's ancestors had done, he had been nothing but kind and helpful. "I use my vegetable garden for the same purpose . . . that and mowing."

He grinned. "Ah yes, the contemplative mow. One of my favorites." He stepped out of the door and gestured inside. "Come in for a minute?"

I smiled and stepped through the threshold only to see a huge stack of boxes waiting for me. "These are *all* your family papers," I said.

"We are clearly packrats," he said. "You will find everything from soup to nuts in there. I've sorted most of it, so hopefully, that'll help." He lifted the lid off one box and showed me the tidy arrangement of expandable folders inside.

"Wow. That's hugely helpful." I leaned closer. "And you labeled everything, too."

"Another tedious habit that keeps me busy." He smiled. "Thanks for looking through these things with your expert eye, Paisley."

I looked up and met his gaze. He looked forlorn, and the

creases around his eyes were deeper than the day before. "It's my pleasure." I smiled. "If it helps, I've only found that the truth of history sets us free, never imprisons us."

Demetrius nodded. "That's my belief, too. I will deal with whatever you find that is hard and painful, and my family will come to terms, too. But to do that, we need to know."

I nodded. "I'll keep you informed every step of the way." I picked up one box. "Better get started."

He helped me load the rest of my hatch and then the backseat. When we slid the last box into the passenger seat next to me, I felt a little overwhelmed. But I reminded myself that I could do this, that I needed to only look at one thing at a time.

I waved as I pulled out of his drive and headed back to Mika's store. I hoped she didn't mind me storing all of this there since I wanted it to be secure but also didn't want to tote it home every night.

Fortunately, Mika was way ahead of me and had cleaned out a corner of her storeroom just for these boxes. So while Sawyer continued his epic nap, we unloaded and got me all set up. Then, I woke up my son because I would need him to go to sleep sometime tonight if I wanted to maintain my sanity.

Sawyer wakes very slowly, so for the next hour, he watched videos and then quietly made God's Eyes with Mika when she wasn't with a customer . . . and I delved in. As much as I was eager to get into Demetrius's family papers, I knew I needed to start with the Benfers because they were more likely to have records relating to Elijah Morris and the property on which the church and manse were built. Plus, experience had taught me that having a framework of names and dates from legal records and records of the enslavers when I started looking at the African American families would help me be able to piece together those stories more easily.

It was kind of ironic, really, but true to history that to be able to research enslaved people you had to first know the stories of those who held them in bondage.

So I took the first box of papers from the Benfers and carefully lifted out a stack. Most of the pages were loose, but I also had pulled out a small journal. I started there. The book was full of thoughts on the weather and planting. I noted a few names of people who were probably enslaved, but by and large the book was mostly useful for someone interested in agricultural history, which was not me. I moved on.

I had made it through most of the first box as Sawyer began to help Mika sort cotton-blend yarn into a rainbow pattern that she'd been wanting to try as a merchandising tactic. My list of first names was growing, but given how often names were repeated during this era, I knew I wouldn't get far if I didn't find more.

Then, on a long sheet of thick paper, I found the break I needed – an inventory of all the people enslaved at BelAirre from 1851 forward. That list alone was wonderful for memorializing the people who had labored there, but for me, it was even more priceless because it listed people by families. Soon, I had three, even four generations in one case, of people, and in two instances, these people were listed with their surnames as well.

I forced myself to finish the box before I moved online to look these families up, just for the sake of consistency and discipline, but soon I had moved all the papers into piles by type and slid the inventory in front of me as I opened my laptop.

Sawyer climbed up in my lap and put his head on my shoulder. "I work, too, Mama," He said. I slid a piece of notebook paper out of my journal and handed him a pen as I put him in the chair next to me. Soon, he was drawing away as I went on the hunt to find Elijah Morris.

It didn't take me long. In 1870, I found Elijah listed as living right next to BelAirre as expected with his mother, Anna, and his wife, Lavinia. His mother was listed as Anna on the inventory I'd found, and so I could identify her there. But it was Elijah's marriage certificate that got my attention, and I immediately called Mika over to show her.

There, he listed his parents, Anna Morris and Nicholas Benfer. "That's Nick's great-great-great-grandfather," I said quietly.

"Whoa," Mika said.

Saw perked up, "What?"

"We just found out who someone's grandfather was, Love Bug."

"Like Boppy is my grandfather?"

"Exactly," I said then turned back to the screen. "Clearly, I need to call Nick and Veronica."

"Yes, definitely, but first, move forward in time, see if you can put Elijah's family tree together." She pointed to the little leaves on the screen that told me there were hints to follow. "That way, you can give them a full picture at once."

"Good idea," I said and began the process of clicking while Mika took Sawyer outside to help her weed the flower boxes at the front of the store. I hoped she had some flowers left when they were done. My son could be a very enthusiastic weeder.

Within a few minutes, I had moved down another generation in Elijah's family, and then another . . . and there I hissed with recognition. Elijah's granddaughter, Elisa Mae married Demetrius Cleveland, the great-grandfather of my friend and the man who was alive when Earnestine Greene died. There was absolutely no way that was a coincidence.

The Benfers, the Morrises, and the Clevelands were all related and not that distantly either.

8

Now, I had a quandary – the information I was finding was relevant to Santiago's investigation, so did I tell him first? Tell Mary since it related to the church and the Monacan burial ground? Or tell the Benfers and Demetrius?

I quickly decided that everyone involved would understand the need for the police to have this information and texted Santiago. "Elijah Morris was a Benfer, and his granddaughter married Demetrius's great-grandfather."

"I'm going to need to see a chart," Santiago said.

"I'm at Mika's. Come over when you can."

"On my way," he said.

I kept adding details to the family tree I was building as I waited for Santiago, but a few moments later, I heard Sawyer squeal and knew that my boyfriend had arrived. The two men in my life came in with Mika close behind, and I was surprised to see Santiago in civilian clothes. He looked great in his uniform, but there was something about him in jeans and a Heinz 57 T-shirt that was even better.

"You're casual," I said.

"I've worked my fair share of hours these past couple of days, so I was hoping we might all be able to take off for the rest of the day and go do something." He winked at me and mouthed the word *swimming*.

I appreciated the covert communication given that the minute Sawyer heard that term there would be no room to say No, but I wasn't inclined to pass anyway. It was blazing hot, I was overwhelmed, and a good swim just might mean that Sawyer would go to bed early even after his epic nap.

"Definitely." I looked over at Mika, who was gathering up Sawyer's craft supplies, and raised my eyebrows.

"Mika, join us for a little time in the water?"

Sawyer perked up at the word water, and said, "We're going swimming?"

"I'd love to, but the store."

I glanced at the clock on my computer. "Miks, it's four-fifteen. Close up forty-five minutes early. Put a sign on the door and tell people you're available by text if they need you." I knew how important keeping solid hours was for my friend, but I also knew that given this heat, she probably wouldn't have any more customers today.

A smile spread slowly across her face. "Okay, but on one condition . . . we get ice cream after." She grinned at Sawyer when he started to jump up and down.

"Let's go, let's go," my little boy said.

"Okay, maybe you and Auntie Miks can get us packed up while I show Santiago something."

Mika nodded, and she and Sawyer began gathering his snack trash and various trucks that had traveled around the store. Santiago sat down next to me and said, "Show me."

I quickly manipulated the family tree on the screen so that Santiago could see the Benfer line and where the Morrises branched off and then where the Cleveland line came in.

"Well, that is something. Have you told them yet?"

I shook my head. "No, I thought you should know first since this might affect your case and things at the church, and I didn't think they'd mind. Everyone seems really focused on telling the whole truth now."

Santiago sighed. "I think so, too, and I do hope we're right . . . and I hope Levi Benfer doesn't get wind of what you've put together here."

"I was actually wondering if he already had. I mean, all of this is public record. He may already know and not want anyone else to find out," I said.

"Well, then we need to let everyone know quickly so that we control the story." He looked over at Sawyer and Mika, who were waiting patiently by the door. "But I expect it can wait until a bit later, don't you?"

I closed my laptop and stood up. "Definitely. Where are we going?"

"Ah, it's a surprise. But before you say we need to stop at your house, I already did, and I have your swimsuits and Sawyer's in the car. I brought both of the ones from your drawer just in case Mika wanted to come."

I stared at him and said, "You went through my underwear drawer?" I wanted to be horrified – and was a little embarrassed – but thoughtfulness always won my heart.

"Just quickly." He kissed my cheeks. "I like the pink ones with the hearts, though," he whispered.

A flush of heat ran up my throat at the thought. "Well, I like those, too," I said when I caught my breath. "Shall we go?"

He laughed and took my hand. "Let's do this," he said loudly enough that Sawyer heard him and headed to the door with Mika grabbing his hand just before he dashed into traffic.

When we arrived at the wide, deep stretch of the Fleur River, Santiago draped a sheet over a branch and stood guard while the three of us changed into our suits. Then, he stripped off his jeans and dove headfirst into the water. I barely had time to get Sawyer's flotation belt on before he followed suit.

Mika and I were a bit more timid on our entries, but soon the four of us were splashing around and skimming rocks across the surface of the water. Our play lasted about an hour, and then we collapsed on the sheet that Santiago spread on the sandy bank and feasted on the cheese and crackers, grapes and nuts that he had brought for dinner.

Then, as Santiago and Sawyer took one last swim, Mika and I stretched out and stared at the sycamore leaves above us. "What do you think the Benfers and Demetrius are going to say?" she asked quietly.

I rolled my head back and forth and let the hard sand rub the last of the tension from the base of my skull. "I don't know, but I think they may actually be excited. They're all so open to finding out the stories of their families . . . Nick's brother, however."

"Yeah," Mika said. "There's always someone who thinks hiding the truth makes it less true."

I laughed. "Isn't that right?"

A couple moments later I heard the telltale cry of a little boy who was running on fumes and had fallen one too many times, and I stood to scoop him into a towel and get him into the car. It was time to go home.

Between the three of us, we were able to keep Sawyer awake all the way back to town and then Santiago offered him a chance to ride in the police car to get to our house. There was no way he was going to doze off with the radio in hand to talk to Savannah, so I took my time gathering my things at Mika's before heading home myself.

When I arrived, Sawyer was already on the couch in his pajamas with chocolate milk and videos. The bedtime routine had started without me, and I felt – for the first time – a sense of real relief that I had someone to help me raise this little boy well. His dad was great with him, but single parenting was exhausting. Santiago's presence was, especially in this moment, such a gift.

With videos done and eye-rubs in full force, I carried my son upstairs with a smile for the man who had moved him directly into our bedtime routine. We read *P Is for Pterodactyl*, and he was asleep before we got to L in the alphabet. Swimming did it every time.

Back downstairs, Santiago had made us tea and gone ahead and set up my laptop and notebook on the trunk in front of the couch. He knew me well, and so he also knew that I wouldn't want to wait to continue this research process I'd begun, especially now that I could loop the Benfers and Demetrius in.

I sat down next to him on the loveseat and snuggled for a minute before I began crafting my email to explain what I'd found, share the link to the tree on the genealogy website, and let them know that I was only beginning but wanted to be sure they were informed of this development.

I also added that I had let the sheriff know about the family relations because it seemed relevant to the work at the church and Earnestine Greene's murder and that he would be in touch if need be.

My hands were shaking just a little as I let Santiago read the message and confirm that it was clear and accurate, and then I hit send and closed the laptop. I knew that if I kept researching or waiting for their responses, I wouldn't sleep later. So while I was aching to keep digging, I needed to be wise.

Plus, there was a very attractive man sitting beside me. I wasn't about to waste that for another moment, and so I turned and planted a kiss firmly on his lips.

THE NEXT MORNING, I woke from a deep sleep and lovely dreams where I was wearing vintage clothes while driving a

Model A car. Sawyer was still sound asleep beside me, and I snuck downstairs with Beauregard padding behind me. It was a rare morning when I got to sip my coffee alone, and I was going to try to take advantage of the time.

Also, something else had bubbled up while I dreamed, and I really wanted to dig into the newspaper archives and see what I could find about Demetrius Cleveland the second, the man who had married into the Morris family and who had been the informant on Earnestine Greene's death certificate.

I fixed my coffee and slipped out onto the front porch, where the morning was unseasonably cool and dry for August. I tucked my laptop onto my legs and pulled up the online newspaper archive of which I was a member. Quickly, I searched for the names "Earnestine Greene" and "Demetrius Cleveland," and I saw the local articles about Bethel Church that Mary had shown me as well as a couple other articles talking about church functions where both of them had been in attendance.

I scanned the headlines for a few minutes and didn't see anything new. So I switched tacks and searched each name individually. That search yielded mostly the same results for Earnestine, a fact I found sad since it seemed most of her life was tied to the church. I hoped she had liked being a pastor's wife.

But the search for Demetrius Cleveland pulled up a lot more. Apparently, he owned the local funeral home that served the black community. His name and Cleveland Funeral Home came up in dozens and dozens of listings. Most of them were obituaries listing Cleveland's as the funeral home handling services, but a few also focused on the man himself.

According to two records, he had been a very generous man who had given a lot of money to location organizations, including two schools for black children in the area. He had also helped found a local soup kitchen that provided meals for families who fell on hard times, and he served as the Worshipful Master of the local Masons here in Octonia.

One article included a photo of him, and he looked stoic and staid in his dark suit with a simple bowtie and side parted hair. Nothing I read about him made me think anything other of him than that he was a good community member, a person his great-grandson and namesake could be proud of.

But I did have one question that was brought up by his profession. So I went back to the genealogy site and searched his name to see if he came up on anyone else's death certificates. I wondered if he might have been the informant on a number of deaths as a funeral director. But it was only Earnestine Greene's record that showed his name, so clearly, he had indeed reported her death because he had some personal connection to it or to the victim.

I sat back and sipped my coffee just as I heard Sawyer begin to stir upstairs. I had about five minutes before he'd be coming down, so I did what I'd been putting off and opened my email.

THE TWO OF us weren't exactly the model of efficiency first thing in the morning, but we did manage to eat, dress, and make it to Mika's shop by ten a.m. Sawyer was super excited because I had packed his backpack full of "work" supplies like white paper, markers, and stickers. His plan was to work next to me all day. I predicted that would last fifteen minutes.

Mika had tidied my work station to her satisfaction, but she knew that the piles of documents I had made needed to remain intact. So they were now stacked neatly in a row against the side of the Cozy Corner. "I kept everything just as it was, simply moved it to keep myself from losing my mind."

I laughed. "I'm sure. And sorry for the mess. I'll keep it tidier. I know it bugs you, and this is your place of business."

Sawyer stood near the stacks, and I could see a gleam of

mischief in his eye. "Don't you think about it, Wild Boy," I grabbed his backpack and set up his workspace. "Let's get to work."

He laughed, moved hesitantly away from the piles of paper, and sat down. "Mama, where's your coffee?"

I smiled at my son, who looked seriously worried. "You're used to me having coffee when I work, huh?"

"Let's go get some. You need it," he said as he put his little hand on my arm.

I grinned. "And you need a chocolate croissant, huh?"

"Yeah!" he shouted.

I smiled at Mika. "Vanilla latte?"

"And a chocolate croissant, please," she said as she added a few skeins of yarn to a bin of beautiful gray.

"You got it. Be back in a minute." I took Saw's hand, and we headed across the street to the coffee shop. The line wasn't long, and within a minute or two, I had placed our order and was waiting by the window as Sawyer played with a puzzle they kept there for just such moments. The sun was streaming through onto his darkening hair, and when it hit his eyes, they glowed a soft gold. Sometimes, his beauty took my breath away.

But that moment of bliss ended abruptly when someone shouted, "Paisley Sutton, you do *not* have my permission to dig into my family's history."

Startled, I grabbed Sawyer and pulled him against me before looking up into the angry face of the person who now stood only a couple of feet away. Levi Benfer.

"Oh, hello Mr. Benfer. I'm sorry. I didn't quite hear you. What did you say?" I had heard him perfectly well, of course, but he was making a scene. The more people who saw this confrontation the better.

"I said," he hissed as he took another step closer to me, "stay out of my family's business. You hear me?"

He stood with his feet spread wide and his hands on his

hips, and the part of me that went to humor in times of fear thought immediately that he was the perfect model of man-spreading in that moment. But the part of me that felt my tiny boy's skull beneath my fingers thought better of saying anything.

"Sir, you will need to take that discussion up with your brother. The research I am doing is at his request with documents he gave me." I picked Sawyer up and took a step away. "Now, please, you are scaring my son."

"Oh, he hasn't seen scared yet." Benfer's voice was low and gravelly. "If you don't stop, you *and* he will know fear, trust me on that."

By now, everyone in the shop was watching, and I just hoped the barista, who was closest, had heard what he said. I took a deep breath and prepared to take my only exit behind the counter with her.

Just then, a large hand clamped onto Benfer's shoulder, and he spun around to see Demetrius Cleveland looming over him. "Sir, kindly leave the woman and her son alone. Now," Demetrius said with authority.

Behind Demetrius, I could see several other people getting up from their tables and coming over to stand beside and behind him. He had been the first to defend me, but he wasn't the only one.

Benfer shook his head slightly and then glanced back at me. "This isn't over," he said before he shook off Demetrius's hand and walked out the door.

I let out a long breath and let myself focus on the image of a villain walking out of a Wild West Saloon that had just flashed into my mind. I needed a mental break for just a second so I could gather myself and tend to Sawyer.

Sawyer was staring over at Demetrius with wide eyes, and I thought at first he was going to cry, but then he grinned. "You're a superhero," he whispered.

Demetrius smiled after glancing at me and seeing I was breathing again. "What would my superhero name be?"

Sawyer tapped his index finger against his cheek in his version of the universal sign for thinking. Then, his eyes lit, and he said, "Iron Claw."

Demetrius threw back his head and laughed. "Excellent. From now on, you know my true identity. But you mustn't tell anyone," he said as he leaned forward and whispered. "I have to keep my superhero nature a secret."

Sawyer nodded seriously. He'd recently watched one of the Spiderman movies with me, and he knew all about secret identities.

"Thank you," I said to Demetrius. I wanted to say a lot more, to thank him for intervening, for helping Sawyer make something wonderful out of a horrible moment. But I didn't want to disrupt this fun or really step back into my fear.

"Of course," he turned to look behind him. "We all saw that, Paisley, so if you need us, I'm going to get everyone's names and numbers for you."

I felt tears pool in my eyes. "Oh, thank you. I wouldn't have even thought of that."

He put his hand on my forearm. "Where can I find you to bring the list?

I pointed across the street. "We're working in Mika's shop today. Thanks again, and I have some information about your family if you'd like to hear what I've found so far," I added.

"Great. See you soon." He turned, took a napkin from the counter, and began to move around the room.

I set Sawyer down and said, "Ready for our chocolate croissants?"

He grinned as I turned to get our order. "I put a couple extra in, my treat," the barista said. "Chocolate always helps."

"Thank you," I said and picked up the drink carrier and the bag.

"I got this, Mama," Sawyer said as he took the bag of pastries and then my hand. "You need to hold my hand because there are lots of cars."

"I do need to hold your hand, Little Man. I really do."

THE REST of the morning was fairly uneventful except for the extreme amount of effort it took for Mika and me to keep tiny, chocolate fingerprints from appearing all over the historical documents.

When Demetrius came over with the napkin list, I thanked him again and showed him what I had found about his great-great-grandfather and asked if he knew. "Know? Of course I know," he said with a smile. "My brother is still a funeral director here in Octonia. One in every generation."

"But not something you wanted to do?" I asked.

"Fortunately, the name and the job aren't inextricably tied. I'm not really built for that kind of constant compassion. It takes its toll on my brother, and he's very good at it. I wouldn't have made it two years." Demetrius shook his head. "No, business is more my strong suit."

"Well, business and," I lowered my voice, "superhero-ing."

He smiled. "That, too." He looked me in the eye. "You're okay, though?"

"I am," I said and meant it. "It's not the first time someone has threatened me, although it is the first time I was warned off of reading old papers." I gestured at the stacks around me on the table.

He scanned the documents. "I sense, though, if I know you at all, that such a threat makes you all the more determined." He winked.

"You know it. If you want me to do something, just tell me I can't." I laughed.

"Well, thank you for what you are doing," he said. Then, he

looked me hard in the eye again. "Paisley, whatever you find about my family, even if it's really awful, you tell the truth, okay? I believe that the truth will set us free."

I nodded and swallowed the lump in my throat. "Okay, I will." I held his gaze steady to back my words.

"Good," he smiled and waved at Mika and winked at Sawyer, who held up his little hand in the shape of a claw, and then Demetrius left with a laugh.

9

The rest of the day passed uneventfully, especially since Mrs. Stephenson came in about noon to watch the store and Mika decided it was a great day to go to the water park in Charlottesville. "You mind if I take Sawyer with me?" she asked with a smirk.

"Well, Sawyer, do you want to go with Auntie Mika to play in the water with other kids?" I couldn't imagine a finer idea of heaven for my son, so I was not surprised when he jumped up and down and said, "Yeah, yeah, yeah."

"Alright, Saw. Let's go. We need to stop by your house and pick up your swimsuit and swim belt."

"And my water shoes," he shouted.

"And your water shoes," she said. "Everything in his room?"

"Actually, it's all in the laundry room, on top of the washer. Shoes are by the door there." I smiled. "Have fun."

"I'll bring him home fed and tired about five-thirty?" Mika said.

"You sure? That's a lot of three-year-old time," I asked.

"Totally sure. See you later." She thanked Mrs. Stephenson

as Sawyer gave the older clerk a high-five, and then they were off.

Mrs. Stephenson was one of those people who could read a room so well that I wasn't surprised that she took out her latest cozy mystery, propped it on the counter, and left me to my work for the afternoon. She attended customers with ease and toodled around to straighten the shelves, only interrupting me to ask if I wanted tea about mid-afternoon, an interruption I greatly welcomed.

"Join me for a cup?" I asked. Ever since Mika had hired the retired accountant to help with the shop, I'd liked the woman. But we didn't get to talk much. Three-year-olds have a tendency to suck all the oxygen and attention in a room.

"I'd love that, if you can spare the time," she said as she set my mug on the table beside me.

"Absolutely." I picked up my mug that read "I See Dead People" and laughed. "Good choice," I said.

"Ever since Mika started doing the Ellery Adams mug thing as well as the shelf enhancers, I've been working hard to pick just the right mug for the right moment." She held hers up. It read, "An Enigma."

I smiled. Mika loved Ellery Adams's mystery novels and the bookstore and coffee shop she ran. In Adams's stories, the owner has a collection of thrift store mugs that she chooses from based on the person who will be drinking from it. I loved that Mika had started that, even if it was just for those of us who worked or knitted here.

"Is it okay if I ask what you're working on?" Mrs. Stephenson asked.

"Of course. It's not a secret." I glanced around. "If it was, I might need to choose a more private workspace." I smiled.

"Good point," she said as she lifted up one of the ledger books next to her. "Do you mind?"

"As long as you keep what you read between us, not at all." I smiled. "I expect you'd be interested in all the bookkeeping I read."

She flipped the pages of the book. "I bet so, even this page is interesting. The ledger notations are fascinating because . . ." she paused and lifted the pages closer to her face, " he's keeping two sets of books here."

"What?!" I said as I stood up and moved to look over her shoulder. She was looking at a ledger from the 1840s. I had already scanned this one to look for names, but as best I could tell, it was simply full of business transactions with other white men in the area. Interesting but not useful for my purposes, at least not that I knew of. "What do you mean he has two sets of books?

She pointed to the "Received" column. "See how he has a number in black ink?"

I nodded.

"But look here, in the shadow, there's a penciled number behind each of these figures. And each one is higher." She moved her finger to the "Expense" column. "Same here but in reverse."

I leaned over. "He's marking down more than what he actually paid in ink? Is that what you're seeing?" I had thought those penciled figures were just the arithmetic of the book, but now that Mrs. Stephenson had noticed this pattern, I couldn't believe I hadn't seen it. "Is he doing something illegal?"

She shook her head. "This is all his money. It looks like he's paying what he actually owed but pretending like he paid more."

"What does that mean? Why would he do that?"

"Well, he could be avoiding paying taxes on all of his income. That's a good possibility." She kept studying the page. "But I can't be sure. It honestly seems like he's hiding how much money he has from someone."

"The state? Or someone closer to home?"

"No way to tell from this, but if you'd like, I can take a look at the financial documents and see what else I find. Maybe get some clues for you?" She looked up at me, and I could see the light of curiosity in her eyes.

"I'd really like that, but let me ask the Benfers. I don't want to violate their trust." I didn't think they'd mind, but I wanted to be sure . . . and I thought I should probably tell them about my encounter with Levi. "Be right back," I said.

I stepped out onto the sidewalk and dialed Veronica's number. She answered on the second ring and said, "You've found something?"

I loved her eagerness, so I said, "Maybe, but I need to ask your permission to have someone else look at the papers, a friend who is a retired accountant."

"Definitely. Totally fine," she said without hesitation. "But care to give me a taste of why?"

I explained about the double entries in the books and how it looked like Nicholas The Fifth might have been underreporting how much money he had actually made and overreporting what he spent. "Not sure why yet, but if my friend can look, she might be able to figure it out."

"Please. Let her see whatever she needs," Veronica said. "That is interesting. I'll talk with Nick and see if that means anything to him."

"Great," I said, and then I took a deep breath. "I do need to tell you one other thing, though."

"Oh, no," she said. "This doesn't sound good."

I related the incident with Levi in the coffee shop and explained how many people had witnessed it. "I don't know what has him so worried, but he's getting a little scary," I said, trying to downplay the real fear I had felt in that moment.

"Paisley, I want you to tell Sheriff Shifflett, and I'm going to have Nick talk to Levi. That is unacceptable, and honestly, none of this is his business. He washed his hands of the farm years ago. Everything here is our personal property, and we can do with it as we wish."

I swallowed. "I'll let Santiago know," I said, "but in my experience, some people really are afraid of the truth. And sometimes the truth can be really painful, traumatizing even."

I heard Veronica breathing and then she said, "You're right. But if Levi is worried about this, he should be talking with us, not attacking you and threatening your son. Please report this to the police, and I will be in touch as soon as Nick talks to Levi."

"Okay," I said. "Thanks."

"We'll be gentle about his concerns, but we aren't going to enable this kind of behavior, Paisley. Please let me know if you have any other encounters with Levi."

I told her I would and hung up. Then, I shook off the fear that had resettled on my shoulders and went back inside.

A beacon of respect, Mrs. Stephenson had left the papers alone and cleaned up our tea mugs, but she was obviously eager to hear what I'd heard, and when I said she could look through things, she let out a little yip of glee.

"When do you want to get started?" I asked.

"Right now," she said as she scooped up the three ledger books I had already reviewed. "I'll work at the counter." She strode over and laid the books carefully by the register. Soon, she was wrist deep in old paper and grinning.

I settled back into my own work and kept recording the names of anyone who was enslaved at BelAirre. It was only when I heard Mrs. Stephenson shout, "Yes," that I realized it was almost five o'clock. Only a few customers had come in, and their purchases had been, it seemed, pretty straightforward. So both of us had worked our way through the afternoon with little interruption.

I jumped up and ran over to the counter. "What did you find?"

"I found the actual numbers," she said in a breathless voice. "The totals, I mean. Look."

She pointed at the end papers at the back of one of the ledgers. I'd looked at what was there, but to me, it looked like more addition and subtraction, the use of any available paper when paper wasn't that available.

"Look here." She tapped her finger beside a long column of numbers that seemed to run down the page and then over into three more columns across the full width of the marbled paper. "These are the same figures from each month in the books. Here, is where he is running his real cash numbers."

I scanned the columns and my eyes landed on the final figure that was written below a horizontal line. "Okay, I see. $16,392. What does that mean?"

"That is, best I can tell, the cash that Nicholas Benfer was putting away under the table, so to speak." She smiled.

"So he was evading taxes?" I sighed. That wasn't going to be a fun fact to share with his namesake.

"Actually, no, I don't think so . . . okay, well, maybe, but I think it was for good reason." She turned to the end paper at the back of the book. There, she read, "Elijah – 16.392."

I grabbed the book from her hands. "Wait, what?"

"It's the same exact figure, although a bit disguised, I think. Why? Do you know this Elijah?"

I ran over to my makeshift desk and pulled up the photo of the image of Elijah and Nicholas that I had taken. "Yes. *This* is Elijah." I tapped his shoulder on the screen, "and *this* is Nicholas Benfer's son."

"Holy crap," Mrs. Stephenson said. "He was giving money to a black man."

"Not just a black man. To one of his slaves," I whispered.

"Whoa," Mrs. Stephenson said. Then she took her phone out of her purse and began to type in numbers. She held up the calculation she had just done. "That's over $165,000 in today's money."

I sat down hard in my chair. I had never heard of such a thing, and I could see why Nicholas had kept it a secret. That kind of generosity to an enslaved man at that time could have gotten him killed. "Please don't tell anyone about this," I said, suddenly quite fearful of what this might mean. Not that I thought someone might kill – at least I didn't think Levi Benfer would kill – but this could change a lot of things about the church and Demetrius's family . . . and well, everyone.

"I won't, Paisley, but when you understand more, you'll explain?" she asked as her eyebrows drew together in concern.

"Absolutely." I studied the ledger now in my hands. "In fact, are you free tonight? I think we need to get some folks together and share this."

"I can be. What time?"

"Eight o'clock at my house. We can talk on the porch while Sawyer sleeps." I needed to get going to meet Mika and Sawyer, but I also knew that I wouldn't be able to concentrate on much else until I shared this with everyone involved.

"Great. I'll bring cookies," she said as she began to total out the register for the day. "See you then."

I nodded as I scooped my computer and the ledger in question into my bag. "You'll look at the other two?" I suddenly asked.

"Already planning on it. I should be able to see the pattern much sooner now if it's there. I'll let you know tonight." Mrs. Stephenson smiled and then stepped over to hug me. "It's going to be okay, dear."

I felt a little of my anxiety ease. "Thanks. I hope so," I said as I put my phone to my ear to call Santiago on my drive home. Thank goodness for Bluetooth.

.   .   .

BY THE TIME I reached home, I had already talked to Veronica, Mary, Demetrius, and Santiago, and everyone, including Chief Stephenson, who Mary was going to call, was going to meet at my house at eight. I knew they might have to wait a bit if Sawyer wasn't ready to sleep, but I was hoping that the water park had made him ready to drop off early.

Sure enough, when Mika pulled in a few minutes after me, she and Sawyer were singing at the top of their lungs, a sure sign that Auntie Miks had employed any tactic necessary to keep the boy awake on the ride home.

I put him on the couch with videos, his blanket, and dinner, and he managed to eat two chicken nuggets, three carrots, and a serving of apple sauce before starting to rub his eyes and demand chocolate milk, the final stage of his bedtime routine.

While Mika tidied the kitchen and took Beauregard for a walk around the yard, I sat with my son and watched him slide toward sleep. About seven, he was on the verge, so I carried him up, read him half of one book, and then tucked him in. He was out by seven-thirty, and I expected when I came up later, he wouldn't have moved a muscle. Thank God for the great invention of water parks.

Back downstairs, I gratefully accepted the large, well-salted margarita that Mika handed me and dropped onto the couch. I had told her the overall sketch on the phone while she was bringing Sawyer home, but now I pulled out the ledger and showed her exactly what Mrs. Stephenson had found.

"So he was sharing his wealth with his friend?" Mika said.

"It appears that way, and a lot of wealth, too." I studied the figures again. "I mean, I love you, but I couldn't even begin to think about giving you over a hundred and fifty thousand dollars."

"What?!" Mika said with mock horror. "Some friend you are."

I smiled. "This begs a lot of questions though. Like why didn't he free Elijah and then give him the money legally?"

Mika nodded. "That's a good question."

We sat quietly sipping our drinks and letting the work of the day drain away. Just before eight, Mika stood, went to the kitchen, and fixed eight more margaritas. I didn't think I needed a second, but when she handed the glass to me and said, "Just in case," I didn't refuse. This might be just the kind of conversation where lowered inhibitions would be helpful. Or not.

I headed out to the porch to direct people around front, where I had set out folding chairs and put out the rockers so that we could sit by the firepit and a little further away from the window near where Sawyer was sleeping. Everyone here knew he was upstairs, but this was going to be a big conversation . . . and big conversations sometimes came with big voices.

Demetrius and Chief Stephenson both turned down margaritas but readily accepted iced tea with mint, and the rest of us added sprigs of mint to our own glasses before settling in. I asked Mrs. Stephenson to explain what she found, and she did so . . . with handouts. I was very impressed.

When she was done, every sat staring at a page from the ledger and then flipping to the copy of the totals page and the note about Elijah that she had copied for them. "I found the same thing in the two other ledgers I have. So far, I calculate that Nicholas gave Elijah the equivalent of about a half million dollars in today's money."

I stared at her and gasped. "Wow."

"Yes, and when you figure that was approximately one third of the entire net worth of Benfer's estate in these three years, well, then you can see he was being profoundly generous with this man."

Mary and Demetrius stared at her and then Mary said, "So this is how Elijah came to own so much land? He bought it?"

Mrs. Stephenson shook her head. "No, I don't think so. I need to see any other documents, but it looks to me," she held up the ledger in her hands, "like Nicholas was actually giving him land quietly under what we'd now call a shell corporation."

Demetrius shook his head. "What are you saying?"

"I'm saying that it looks like Nicholas gifted your ancestor over two hundred acres of land and a half million dollars." Mrs. Stephenson's face was serious, but I could see the glint of glee in her eyes. She loved this story.

"Well, way to go, Grandpa Nicholas," Nick Benfer said. "Nothing, short of him having freed all his slaves, could make me prouder." He looked a little choked up.

Chief Stephenson spoke. "It is a great gift, and I don't want to bring down the mood. But he didn't free Elijah. Why not?"

Demetrius cleared his throat. "I may know the answer to that. Here in Virginia, if someone was freed, they had two years to leave the commonwealth. They couldn't stay here and remain free."

I tilted my head. "Yes, I do remember that. Passed the legislature in 1806, I think. Some people hated it because it split up families, but those with the power did it to prevent revolt and escapes, right?"

"Right. On my dad's side, his great-grand-uncle got freed, but he had to leave his entire family behind because the master didn't free them. He never recovered and basically drank himself to death in Harrisburg, Pennsylvania." Demetrius's face was grim. "Freedom came at a great cost."

I sighed. "So you're thinking that Elijah didn't want to be freed because his family was here, and he didn't want to leave?"

Demetrius nodded. "I think it's a possibility."

The circle was very quiet. "I'll dig into that and see what I can find about Elijah's family, see if I can determine the reasons Benfer gave him that gift," I said.

"Thank you, Paisley," Demetrius said.

"Yes, thank you," Nick added.

Santiago cleared his throat. "We also need to talk about your brother, Nick." I could tell that Santiago wasn't really eager to have this conversation, but I knew he needed to.

"Yes, we do," Nick said. "I'm glad Paisley told you what happened."

Demetrius, Mary, and Chief Stephenson passed a confused look among them. "Why, what happened?" Mary asked.

"Levi threatened me." I swallowed, "*and* Sawyer if I didn't stop this research." I explained what had happened in detail, and, not surprisingly, everyone was horrified.

"Can you arrest him, Santiago?" Mika asked.

"I could," he said, "but that might cause more trouble than it's worth since it would mean formal charges and a trial and—"

I interrupted. "I don't want to press charges," I said firmly. "I just want him to understand he can't speak to me or my son that way." I shivered. "He needs to know that Sawyer is protected."

"I spoke with him this afternoon and let him know in no uncertain terms that he was to leave you alone," Nick said. "I also asked my attorney to send him a formal cease and desist letter that lays out exactly why he has no right to interfere."

Santiago smiled. "Now, you're talking, Nick. That's perfect."

I blushed. "Thank you so much."

Veronica leaned over and took my hand. "No need for thanks. It's simply the right thing to do. We don't want anyone threatening our friends, and, selfishly, we want you to be clear-headed enough to really do this research well. It's important."

I leaned over and tossed another log onto the fire while I said a silent prayer of gratitude for good people in my life. "Thanks, everyone."

We enjoyed the dance of the flames for a few minutes, and

then I decided to see if I could recruit some help with this research. I was the only one really qualified and trained to go through the documents, but my friends had other skills. I took a deep breath and took command, channeling my best Jean-Luc Picard energy.

"I could use some help," I said and as every head in the circle nodded, I began to dispatch my requests. "Mary, could you dig through the church records to see what you can find about Elijah's gift of land for the church? See if there are any papers or such?"

"You got it, woman," Mary said.

"Demetrius, can you do the same for your family's papers?"

He smiled and nodded.

"Santiago, can you ask the clerk's office to help you put together a chain of title for that land and all of the Benfer land over the years? I'd like to see if we can track the land's movements over the years."

Santiago laughed. "You want me to use my power for good?"

"I do," I smiled.

"You got it." He squeezed my hand.

"Mrs. Stephenson, can you help me continue to go through the records to find more anomalies like this one?" She clapped her hands and grinned, so I took that to be a yes.

Finally, I looked at Chief Stephenson. "I hate to ask something of you given all that you are managing right now, but could you continue to see what you can find about that land in your tribal records?"

"Absolutely, Paisley," she said. "I am eager to see if Elijah knew people were buried there or if, perhaps, he donated the land with the idea that it would be preserved."

I studied her face a moment as I thought about that. "You think he might have been protecting the land by giving it to the church?"

"I think it's a possibility. Maybe he didn't trust that he could keep it himself or that If It passed down to his children they would remember and honor the burial ground there." She shrugged. "I'm hoping that's the case, I guess." She looked over at Demetrius and smiled.

Orders dispatched, I refrained from saying "Make it so" and instead said, "Thank you."

Then, Mika cleared her throat. "And what are my marching orders, Paisley?" Her voice was small.

"I have the most important job of all for you . . . Sawyer duty. I'm going to put my nose to the grindstone for the next few days, and I could use your help to keep that little boy occupied. Do you mind?"

Mika beamed. "I'd love that! I have about a million ideas for what we can do at the store. Maybe I'll even have a kids' class at the end of the week."

I could see the metaphorical wheels turning behind everyone's eyes, and I took the last sip of my margarita in a sort of quasi-contentment. We had a lot of questions to answer, but I knew we could do it. At least I hoped we could.

10

The next morning as soon as I got Sawyer settled in at Mika's store, I walked up to the historical society office and knocked on the door. Technically, they weren't open on Thursday mornings, but I'd asked Xzanthia Nicholas, the director, if we could meet anyway. She readily agreed when I told her it was about the church, and now, she was standing there, elegant as usual, with her glowing, walnut-colored skin and her long, golden triangle earrings.

"Paisley, I've been pulling some documents that might be useful," she said as she gestured for me to come in. "I know the last thing you probably need is more documents to go through, but well, this is what we do, isn't it?"

I smiled. "Yes, ma'am, it is. Thank you."

We sat down at the long table in their archival reading room, and she pulled over the first box. "This is our collection of things about the church. I expect they have much more, as they should, but if there's something here that they might not have, I thought I'd get it out for you."

I flipped through the folders, which appeared to be mostly old bulletins and funeral programs, a couple of fans with the face of white Jesus on them, which made both Ms. Nicholas and I shake our heads. I couldn't see anything of particular import here, but I wasn't the expert. "Do you mind if Mary Johnson comes over and looks through this box? She's the church historian, and she'll know what isn't duplicated in their records. Maybe you all can even coordinate a bit."

"Perfect," Ms. Nicholas said as she slid the box away and grabbed another. "This here is our Benfer collection. We have other pieces on display in the museum here, but I reviewed those and they don't have any mentions of enslaved people or anything about land in specific. You can browse those if you want, but I thought this might be more useful."

I stood to look through the boxes contents. "Oh, this is correspondence and," I paused as I carefully lifted out a folder marked "Will," "what is this?"

I sat down and gingerly laid the folder open as I began to read, "I, Nicholas Benfer, being of sound mind and body do, on this day, 1 July 1852, leave this final will . . ."

"This is Nicholas Benfer's will." The blood was pounding in my ears. "But not the final one, an earlier one, right?"

"I believe so," she said. "You can tell me more certainly, but given that this one isn't signed by the clerk, I don't think it was ever filed officially."

"So it's probably a draft." I scanned down the page, looking for the upswing of capital letters to indicate names. About two-thirds of the way down the page, I saw it, "Elijah Morris," and I slowed my eyes.

"I do bequeath to my brother-at-heart, Elijah Morris, half of all my earth possessions and leave to him his wife, Lavinia, and his children Moses and Ned."

I sat back hard against my chair as I passed Ms. Nicholas the paper and let her read for herself. "Whoo!," she said. She knew the importance of that sentence, and the danger of it too. "That's not in the final version?"

I shook my head. "No, but there is more." I explained to her about how Nicholas The Fifth had given all that money to Elijah over the years but hidden it.

"Because he had to," she said with a shake of her head. "He couldn't give him all of this property without freeing him and his family, but if he freed them, they had to leave."

I stared at her for a second. "But you're right, if he could bequeath his wife and children to him, he must have owned them. So why not free them all?"

"That's a good question," Ms. Nicholas said. "Let's find out." She pulled another folder from the box, and I saw the tab was labeled "Inventory."

"An inventory of enslaved people at BelAirre? No way."

"Indeed. It was the document I was most interested to find in here. It's rich with information, including family groupings and some occupations." She slid a stapled pair of pages over to me. "I already made you a copy, but I thought you might want to see the original first."

I smiled and said, "Yes, please." Then, I scanned the document. It was dated 1852, a year after the earlier inventory I'd found but organized by families as the other one had been. There, I saw Elijah and Lavinia Morris and their children Moses, Ned. Emily, "Elijah's sister." "Elijah had a sister."

Ms. Nicholas nodded. "And see that note next to her name."

I drew my eyes right and saw there, in parentheses, the phrase, "At the Beazleys." I looked up at Ms. Nicholas. "She's not at BelAirre." I felt my heart sink.

"That's what I'm thinking. The Beazley plantation was next door, so it sounds like she was there for some reason." Ms. Nicholas sat back and looked at me.

"And if she was with them, she might have been owned by them, somehow, and that would mean that Elijah would have to leave her behind if he was freed." I choked back tears. "What a terrible choice."

Mrs. Nicholas nodded. "Absolutely terrible. The question we have to answer is why she was there."

"I mean if she was born to Lavinia, then she was technically the property of Nicholas Benfer, right?" I knew the answer to my own question, but this situation was so strange that I was questioning what I knew.

"Correct. So why was that not the case?"

"Or why was a tiny baby – she had to have been born in the last year because she's not on the inventory from earlier that year," I told her, "living away from her family."

"Sounds like you have another mystery, my dear." Ms. Nicholas slipped the folder back into the box and closed the lid. "I'm going to leave these right here so you can come back, but I can see from that look in your eye that you need to track down this story first."

I sighed. "Yeah. I do." I stood up. "Thank you." I bent down to give the tall woman a hug. "I'll keep you posted."

"Please do," she said as she stood and walked me to the door. "And be careful, Paisley. Even one-hundred-seventy-five-year old secrets sometimes get people scared."

Didn't I know it?

I CALLED Santiago as I walked back toward Mika's store to check on Sawyer, and he answered in a whisper. "I'm in the clerk's office. Call you back in ten?" he said.

"Or just come to Mika's. I have something to tell you, too. Oh, and see if you can find any legal cases involving the Benfers in the 1850s," I added at the last minute.

"Okay. That sounds interesting."

"Very," I said before hanging up. Everything about this situation was interesting and hard and beautiful and complicated, but I was determined to sort things out, somehow.

The piece I couldn't figure out how to make sense of was the

Monacan burial ground. Why would Elijah Morris give ground to the church if he knew that there were burials on it? Did he know there were burials on it? Did he not care? Or did he, as the Chief had suggested, want to protect it? So many questions.

But I put them all aside when I walked in and saw my three-year-old completely wrapped up in yarn like a mummy and his auntie laughing hysterically as he walked around groaning and running into things with his outstretched arms. "Oh, Mummy Sawyer, your mummy is here," I said with a chuckle.

"Mummy, oooh," Sawyer said as he pivoted and began to waddle toward the sound of my voice, which was unfortunately behind a tower of crates full of yarns. Both Mika and I lunged to catch him, but we were too late and all the crates tumbled, leaving him in a pile of fuchsia and teal yarn.

I quickly pulled the crates off and prepared to comfort my son after he had been hit on the head, but when I got to his yarn-covered face I could hear the delightful peals of his laughter. Between snorts and laughs, he said, "I'm buried in my tomb again."

We'd watched a special on Egypt a few days ago, and as usual, my son had picked up more than I had known he did. "Yes you are, Mummy Sawyer. Are you going back to your eternal rest?"

He jumped out and said, "No way, Mama. I want to curse people." He blindly climbed his way out of the pile and began wandering around the shop again as Mika and I picked up the yarn and made a stack of the crates closer to the wall.

For the next few minutes, we let Sawyer chase one or the other of us around the shop, and the customers that came in loved it. One women so loved the color that Sawyer was "wearing" that she bought out the rest of Mika's stock. "Now that's a marketing technique I never would have considered," Mika said after the woman left.

I laughed but then let my smile fall away as I saw a grim-faced Santiago come in. He looked downright upset, and I instantly knew we needed to talk without a mummy's interruption. "Sawyer, Mummy is going to get her little mummy a treat. Chocolate croissant or cherry danish?" I asked.

"Cherry croissant," he said with a laugh.

"Fair enough. Both it is," I said and hoped my easy agreement would make my leaving equally easy. Fortunately, Mika had a new idea up her sleeve, and as Santiago and I walked back out of the store, I heard her say, "Do you want to be Frankenstein's monster next?"

"Yeah!" Sawyer shouted, and all thoughts of me leaving were banished.

As we crossed the street, I took Santiago's hand and said, "You okay?"

He glanced over at me. "Yeah. Just what I found is terrible. Let's sit down first, okay?"

I took a deep breath. If Santiago, the sheriff who had seen all manner of horrible things, needed to sit down to tell me something, I knew I wasn't going to like it. "Sure," I said and squeezed his fingers.

We ordered our coffees and sat down at a table in the back corner at Santiago's request. He apparently didn't want a lot of attention right now.

He took a sip of his coffee and then pulled out his phone. "The clerk's staff is making copies of the documents for me as we speak, but I wanted to give you this information ASAP."

"Okay," I said, my heart starting to race. "What is it?"

"In 1851, David Beazley filed a suit against Nicholas Benfer for three thousand dollars claiming that Benfer had harvested from ten acres of his land for the past five years and, thus, owed him at least that much for the wheat he had stolen."

"Okay, that's weird. These guys usually knew the means and bounds of their land pretty clearly. Why would Benfer farm someone else's land?" This wasn't making much sense to me.

"Well, that was the heart of the dispute. Benfer claimed the land was his and showed the land grant boundaries to prove it, but Beazley claimed that Benfer's father had sold that land to his father twenty some years before in 1824. He even produced documents to that effect." Santiago sighed.

"So Benfer was wrong?" Seemed odd that a father wouldn't tell his son exactly what land he was inheriting, but given that I'd never inherited anything, what did I know.

"Apparently, but there's more. It seems the original purchase of land was a kind of trade." He took a deep breath. "Land for people."

I swallowed. "Benfer bought an enslaved person with land." I knew this kind of thing had happened, but still, hearing about it always made my stomach turn.

"And a promise was secured by Benfer. If he sold Beazley the land, Beazley would give up his claim to five acres at the top of the BelAirre plantation."

I gasped. "Where the church is?" I could feel the tumblers of this big puzzle sliding into place.

"Exactly where the church is." He took my hand. "Here's the really intense part."

"There's something more intense than all this?" I asked.

"The person Benfer bought with that land in 1824 was Elijah Morris's mother, Anne." Santiago held my gaze and watched as I saw the last piece drop and the lock of history open.

"So Anne was bought from Beazley in order to protect the Monacan burial ground? Is that what you are telling me?" I was a little breathless with it all.

"I believe so." We both sat and stared at the table for a few moments as all this sank in. I couldn't help but wonder if there was more.

I took another deep breath and said, "Okay, so here's another piece of this puzzle that we need to figure out. For some reason, Beazley comes to own Elijah's sister, Emily, when she's just a tiny baby and Emily is Anne's daughter."

Santiago frowned and asked me to explain, so I told him what Ms. Nicholas and I had found in the 1852 inventory and about the draft of Nicholas The Fourth's will.

"This is all getting so complicated," he said and then took a long swig of his coffee. "But I think we need to assume that Earnestine Greene figured at least some of this out."

"More than just that there was a burial ground under their manse?"

He shrugged. "Maybe. It seems like if she was looking into things, she might have figured out far more than we knew."

I nodded. "Okay, so I will keep digging, and now I have another job for Mika – reviewing Earnestine's journal for information about the Beazleys."

Santiago pulled me to my feet. "And I need to go talk to Hortense Beazley." He stopped short and looked over at me. "Levi Benfer's girlfriend," he said pointedly.

I could almost see the flash of insight as it sparked in his brain. "What?! Who is Hortense Beazley?"

"The current owner of Magnolia, the Beazley plantation next to the Benfers."

"And she's dating Nick Benfer?"

Santiago nodded. "Has been for years, decades even. They're not here a lot because they travel for most of the year, but they've been together since high school."

I flashed back through my high school memories, but given that I was distinctly middle class, very bookish, and content to do my marching band thing, I just didn't run in the circles that the Benfers and Beazleys had. Plus, I guessed they were a few years older than me, which meant I probably didn't know them anyway.

"This is getting more and more weird," I said.

Santiago wrapped his arm around my waist as we crossed the street again. "Yes. Yes it is."

AS SOON AS I got back to Mika's store and gave her the brief version of what we learned, I texted my dad and Lucille and asked if they could come take Sawyer for the afternoon. Mika was eager to get back into the journals, and with Mrs. Stephenson coming to staff the shop, we could go to my house with everything and spread out.

Dad and Lucille were going to take Sawyer to the children's museum downtown and then out for hamburgers, and so we'd have several hours to work in quiet. And I knew Saw would love all the hands-on things at the museum. Plus, French fries were this guy's love language.

Soon, he was off with glee, and I was glad to see we might be moving into a stage where departing from me wasn't so painful for him, especially since he was going to start morning preschool in a few weeks. And to be honest, while I adored my son, I did enjoy time away from him so that I could concentrate and not worry that he might impale himself on something.

Mrs. Stephenson came in all abuzz with excitement, and I braced myself for more news. I didn't know how I was ever going to process all this information and make it make sense in my brain, but she was so eager to share that I couldn't ask her to wait, even though I thought I might understand more if she did.

Instead, the three of us sat down in the Cozy Corner, and she told us that after going through all of Nicholas The Fifth's ledgers, she found that he had left almost half a million dollars' worth of cash to Elijah. ("Updated for our dollar value today, of course," she added.)

I fluttered my lips. "Wow. I wonder how much of Benfer's estate that was?"

"Ahead of you on that one," Mrs. Stephenson said with a smile. "I am curious, too, so I'm tallying what I can from his ledgers and the rough property values I can find online." She tapped the laptop case on her knee. "If we don't get too busy," she smiled at Mika, "and I hope we are too busy – I should know by the end of the day."

"Thank you so much," I said. "You are amazing."

She blushed. "Actually, I think I may start a third career as a forensic accountant," she said with a laugh. "Part-time yarn affi-cionado, part-time investigator. Sounds pretty exciting to me."

Mika laughed. "You can always do your investigating on my clock."

I stood and picked up one of the Benfers' boxes. "We're off, then," I said.

"Call if you need anything," Mika added as she hefted her own box and headed out the front door to my car. We quickly loaded the rest of the papers, including Demetrius's family files and then headed to my house, by way of the pizza parlor for an extra-large, extra cheese to fuel us through the day.

After scarfing down a couple pieces each, we washed the grease off our fingers and got to work at the kitchen table. Mika had ordered Earnestine's journals chronologically and was reviewing our notes as she scanned the pages. Every once in a while, she'd jot something down and then keep going. She was a person who liked to work through a problem all the way before talking about it, so I left her to the work as best I could.

However, since I process information verbally, I did find it hard to not interrupt her every few minutes when I found something new. Still, even with my intermittent outbursts of info, we made good progress through the afternoon.

By five p.m., I had a pretty solid spreadsheet of all the names I'd found, so far, in the Benfer papers, and I had created a good and as comprehensive as possible family tree for Demetrius's ancestors back to about 1845, complete with notes and dates from his family archives. But so far, I had just assembled data. I hadn't yet begun to make connections, and that was going to be the rich part.

This assembling of the skeleton of info had to be done first. Otherwise, I wouldn't be able to form stories from the various anecdotes I could collect.

Across the table, Mika was on her last journal. She'd skimmed most of it, using my tip about looking for capital letters to find proper names, and her notes about the Beazleys took up a couple of pages. I was so eager to hear what she learned, but I gave her space and began to look into the Benfer papers for more information.

I scanned the correspondence but didn't see much beyond the usual talk about the weather, travel, and high-society gossip. I did take my time, though, when I came across a sheaf of documents that were signed with Nicholas Benfer's name. A quick check of the dates confirmed that this was Nicholas the Second, Nicholas the Third and Elijah's father, and I delved in.

My attention paid off quickly on the third page as I read what was clearly Nicholas The Third's journal entry from 1824:

TODAY, *I bought Anne from Beazley. It was crucial I get her, a request from my beloved Wilmington. I didn't mention a thing to Beazley about what we knew, and he seemed none the wiser. He got a good land deal, and I hope that will satisfy.*

BELOW THAT PARAGRAPH WAS AN ENTRY, *Anne – $400.*

I HUNG MY HEAD. I didn't know exactly what Nicholas meant about what he and his wife Wilmington knew about Anne, but I could guess . . . and I didn't want to think about it much. I flipped the page and read on to find his entry from three months later.

BEAZLEY HAS DISCOVERED the truth and is determined to get his fair due since he seems to believe we knew about Anne's condition. We did, of course, after our house girl, Kessiah, told Wilmington and asked for our help. But we will not tell him that, and he cannot prove it. I am just glad mother and child are safe.

MY MOUTH WAS DRY, and I felt a little nauseated. Benfer had bought Anne and her child because Anne was pregnant. He seemed to be trying to do a good thing, but I wasn't able to get past the systems and processes that made the purchase of people possible at all. I couldn't get the image of a pregnant young woman being traded like a piece of furniture, no matter how good the intention behind the purchase.

So, Anne was pregnant with Elijah. When the Beazleys finally realize this, they sue and end up with baby Emily as "payment" for only having one enslaved person in the original exchange when Anne was actually pregnant when she was "sold" for the land. So, Emily becomes a Beazley.

I stood and went to pour myself a glass of wine. I needed it, and from the look on Mika's face – she was pale and wan – I thought she probably needed one, too. When I put the glass down beside her notes, she looked up, closed the final journal and sat back. "Thanks," she said and took a long pull from the glass. "I so need this."

"Me, too," I said as I sipped my own chardonnay. "You want me to go first or do you want to?"

"Let me because I think I need to be sure I'm understanding correctly." She stood. "But can we do this on the couch. I need comfy seating before we go on."

I laughed. "Of course, and how about some hummus and pita chips?" When she smiled, I grabbed the bag from the cabinet and the tub from the fridge and followed her to the love seat.

With the snacks between us, she told me what she'd found. "As best I can tell, Earnestine suspected some secret that the Beazleys were keeping and that the Morrises felt obligated to keep, too. She keeps talking about Nicholas Benfer and Elijah Morris's mother, but she never says anything explicit. I get the sense that she knows what the secret is but doesn't feel like it's safe to say."

I sighed. "That would make sense. It could have put her in danger. Other people, too." After another long sip of my wine, I told Mika about what I've found, and as I talked, she scooped one chip after another into the hummus and then to her mouth. I understood the urge. This was the kind of news that involved good food.

"So the Beazleys and the Morrises are somehow related. That's what we're saying, right?"

I nodded. "I think so, and it sounds like Earnestine Greene had figured that out, too. I wonder if that was part of what she told the deacon board that day."

Mika sat back and finished her wine. "That reminds me. I've been thinking. If the Deacons were the only ones who knew what she did, doesn't her killer have to be one of them?"

"Well, that's a good point," I said and wondered why I hadn't considered it before. "But do we know she didn't tell anyone else?"

Mika stood and headed to the kitchen, coming back momentarily with the wine bottle from the fridge. After she filled our classes, she sat back down and said, "I guess that's what we might need to figure out."

My phone rang, and I scooped it up from the coffee table. Lucille. "Hi," I said. "How's he doing?"

"Well, he's doing great, actually, and he wants to know if he can stay the night with Baba and Boppy." Lucille sounded anxious, but I wasn't sure if that was because the thought of having her grandson at her house in the wee hours of the morning was frightening or because she was worried about me.

"That's exciting," I said, "and it's fine with me. But do you mind if I talk with him to be sure we're all clear on what that means?"

"I was hoping you'd say that," Lucille said with a laugh. "Here he is."

"Hi Mama. I'm going to sleep with Boppy okay?"

I chuckled. "Does Boppy know you're going to sleep with him?"

"Yeah," he said. "See you tomorrow." Then he hung up.

Lucille called right back and said, "Well?"

"Sounds to me like he wants to have a slumber party with his Boppy. That okay with you?"

"Totally fine with me. I'll sleep in the guest room." She laughed. "We'll bring him over in the morning?"

"I'll swing by and pick him up. Thanks so much, and don't let him con you into too much sugar or too late a bedtime."

Lucille cackled. "Are you kidding? That little boy is going to bed by seven-thirty because both of us are going to need to be asleep by eight. Whew!"

"Good plan. See you in the morning." I hung up and swigged most of my glass of wine. My son was safe and happy, and we had a mystery to solve. Well, three mysteries.

"Okay, so let's make a list," I said. "What are we trying to figure out?

Mika picked up a notepad and pen from the table beside the couch and wrote as she said, "1. Was Nicholas Benfer the Fourth Elijah Morris's father with Anne?"

"Right, that's the big question. 2. Why is Emily Morris living at the Beazley place in 1852? I think it is because the Beazleys have done the math and realize when Anne went to the Benfers in exchange for the land, she was pregnant. They thought the 'trade' was for one person, but there was a baby."

Mika wrote that down and added, "3. Did Elijah Morris know about the Monacan burial ground by the church? 4. Who did Earnestine Greene tell about what she knew?"

"And 5. Who knows what now?" I added. "Gracious, no wonder we're tired. This is a lot."

A knock at the door brought us both to our feet as I went to answer and Mika took the wine bottle to the recycling bin. Santiago stood with his own bottle of wine at the door, and when I invited him in, he said, "Thought we might need this."

Mika laughed. "We just finished one, but yes, we do." She opened the bottle, got out a third glass, and poured us all generous portions.

Then, we took our seats around the table, somehow knowing we needed to be fully committed to this conversation. I was eager to tell Santiago what Mika and I had learned, but I even more badly wanted to hear what his conversation with Hortense Beazley had brought about.

"I didn't learn much except that it was definitely Hortense who sent Nick Benfer to talk to you. She didn't deny that, and she didn't seem ashamed of it either."

I rolled my eyes. Bullies infuriated and exasperated me. "But she didn't say why?"

"Nope, couldn't get her to admit anything except that she was livid that Nick had gotten his lawyer involved." Santiago's faced opened into a wide smile. "I kind of liked that part of the conversation."

I sighed. "Well, we may not need to know what she's trying to hide because we may have figured it out ourselves." I looked over at Mika and nodded.

She went through, methodically, and told Santiago everything we'd discovered from the purchase of Elijah's mother when she was pregnant with him to what it looked like Earnestine Greene knew, and she landed the story perfectly by saying, "So we think that the Beazleys are actually kin to the Morrises because they took baby Emily."

Santiago sipped his wine slowly and then looked at me. "Wow."

"I know, right?" I said. "Here's the list of questions it seems like we need to answer. Obviously, we're just trying to stick with the research part, but these may also help you in your investigation, too.?

He read through the list and nodded. "I have a similar list, but I also need to tell you something else." He sighed and took my hand while looking at Mika. "Hortense said that if we pried into her family's history she was going to get a restraining order against anyone involved."

I laughed. "She can't do that. This information was freely given from the owners. She has no case."

Santiago sighed. "But she does have an uncle who is a judge."

I groaned. I loved living in my small town, where everyone knew everyone. Most of the time. But when the nepotism got going, it could really feel like a fair shot was a mystical thing. "Ugh. So what do we do?"

Mika didn't hesitate. "We do the right thing. We find our answers. We tell the truth. We refuse to be bullied."

I so loved my best friend. So loved her.

11

We had just begun to brainstorm our next steps, inspired by Mika's mini-speech, when her phone rang. "It's Mrs. Stephenson," she said.

As Mika stepped outside to take the call, Santiago looked at me and asked, "Don't you all know that woman's first name. Why do you all talk to her so formally?" He smiled.

"Old-fashioned, I guess. But yes, her first name is Lizzie. She hasn't corrected us yet when we call her Mrs. Stephenson, so I assume she prefers it."

Santiago rolled his eyes. "The Southern ways die hard, don't they?"

"Yes, sir, they do," I said with an emphasis on the *sir*.

He leaned over and kissed me before saying, "Enough of that, you." I kissed his cheek and got up to pour more wine. I had a good twelve hours before I needed to sober up, so I was going to take full advantage.

I had just set our now full-again glasses down when Mika came back in. Her eyes were wide, and she looked a little flushed.

"Wow, that must be some news," I said.

"It is," she said breathlessly. "By Mrs. Stephenson's calculations, Nicholas Benfer gave Elijah Morris more than half of the value of his estate in cash."

I set down my wine glass. "More than half? Is that what you said?"

Mika nodded, and I blew a hard blast of air out of my mouth. "Holy cow."

"I think I know the answer to this, but that's rare, right?" Santiago asked.

"Not just rare," I said, "unprecedented." My mind was buzzing with all this news meant. I had a lot to say about this in a lot of ways, but first, we had to solve these mysteries. Then, we could confront the wonder and the continued horror of Elijah's situation. "We need to tell everyone."

Mika agreed. "Mrs. Stephenson is going to open for me tomorrow, so maybe we can get everyone else together at the church and talk through things."

I looked at my phone. It was almost nine o'clock, but for news this important, I didn't think anyone would mind a late phone call.

The three of us divvied up our list of calls, and within a few minutes, everyone who needed to know was invited to meet at the church at eight-thirty the next morning. I called Lucille and checked on Sawyer, who was now asleep with his Boppy in his grandparents bed, and then I asked her if they could keep him until about ten in the morning. She readily agreed and then asked if there was an update. I filled her in, and she said, "Just let us know if we need to plan another day of activities. Actually, I'm going to go ahead and get a plan together. Just in case."

I loved my stepmother. "Thank you, Lucille."

I hung up, and then Santiago offered to give Mika a ride back into town. Normally, I would offer to let her stay here, but I kind of wanted a couple of hours to just think by myself. I knew Mika wouldn't mind if I sewed while she was here, but I didn't want to feel guilty for just picking a show I loved and diving in without conversation.

"I'll see you in the morning," I said to her and gave her a hug. "Get a good night's rest."

"Are you kidding? With this much wine in me, I'll be lucky to be conscious when we get to town." She laughed.

Santiago looked at me in feigned horror and then turned to Mika. "You know I can't carry you up those stairs to your apartment, right?"

"No problem. Just get me to the landing, and I can sleep there." They were both laughing as they left.

I sat down and pulled out my sewing basket. I was about two-thirds done with Sawyer's bulldozer, and I was hoping that I could finish it tonight. The pattern was so simple and monochromatic that it seemed feasible, and when I tuned into the first episode of *The Vampire Diaries* spin-off, *The Originals*, I was hooked. I set an alarm for midnight just so that I'd remember to go to bed and not binge and stitch all night.

My alarm wasn't needed, however, because by eleven I was zonked. So I packed up the stitching, turned off the TV, checked on Beau's water, and then carried him up to bed with me. He promptly took over two-thirds of the queen, and my hopes for a luxurious and spread-out night's sleep without my son were vanquished.

Still, I slept well, except for the dreams. I was trapped in a huge plantation house, and no matter how many doors I went through, I never could find my way out. It was awful, and I woke up all sweaty and out of breath.

Fortunately, it was almost seven, so I got out of bed, grabbed a shower, and made myself a good breakfast of eggs, cheese, and avocado. I was going to need stamina today, so I also prepared a second French press of coffee. No need to skimp on the caffeine when this much needs to be figured out.

By the time I left for Mika's shop, I felt ready, or at least as ready as I could be for something I couldn't predict. On the drive over, I put on my '90s mix and let The Cure and Rusted Root carry me into town.

When I arrived at the church, everyone was already there and sampling the donuts that Demetrius had bought from the Mennonite truck that parks downtown on Fridays. I thought about foregoing the treat, especially since I wasn't hungry, but quickly told myself I'd be rude if I didn't partake, so I grabbed a cruller. It was delightful, all airy and light.

Someone had already put out a circle of chairs near the hole where the manse had formerly been, and slowly we all chatted as we made our way to the seats. The energy around us was sharp and quick. Everyone was on edge.

Santiago explained what we had found about Anne and Emily and the Beazleys, and then I explained how the land deal had contained a clause related to the land near the church. Finally, Mika told everyone what Mrs. Stephenson had found.

When we finished, everyone looked a little stunned, and it was quiet for a few minutes as the information sunk in. Then, Chief Stephenson said, "So Nicholas Benfer," she glanced over at Nick, "your great-great-grandfather was trying to protect this land?"

I looked at Nick and nodded. "It appears that way. The question we have is about Elijah and whether or not he knew about the burial ground here when he donated the land."

Mary spoke up. "I think I can answer that. Yes, I believe he did." She explained that she had spent yesterday afternoon going through the records at the historical society with Ms. Nicholas. They had found the Bill of Gift for the land, and in it, there was a clause that stated the land to the south side of the church building could never be modified or built upon. "He mandated that the burial ground be intact," Mary finished.

"Why didn't he explain that there was a burial ground?"

Demetrius asked. "If he'd said that, no one would have possibly thought of building there." He sounded a little annoyed.

"I don't know," Mary said. "Maybe he didn't know."

"Or maybe," Chief Stephenson said, "he didn't tell anyone because he knew what we know now – people raid Indian graves all the time. He must have thought his stipulation would protect it well enough."

I sighed. "Well, that answers one question and brings up another. Why did the church violate that agreement?"

Demetrius sighed. "I expect no one knew about the agreement. The land was given about twenty years before the manse was built. It's possible the information was lost in time."

Mika sighed. "That seems possible, but it's still tragically sad. And," she added, "it doesn't answer the question of why the church didn't take action when Earnestine Greene told them about the burial ground."

Mary responded again. "That's a good question, and I hope to dig back into more records today to find out the answer. I'll let you know what I find." She looked over at Demetrius. "Want to help?"

"No, thank you." He turned to Chief Stephenson. "Respectfully, Chief, do we really need to squirrel our way into this information? After all, we are honoring the burial ground now. Isn't that what's best?"

Chief Stephenson sighed. "It's best for us, but for you, for your congregation, I think you need to know. We need nothing further than what is already being done, but the truth is a gift. I think your people need that gift."

Demetrius frowned and sat back in his chair. He looked markedly unhappy.

"Sorry to change the subject," Veronica Benfer said, "But is there a way to know for sure that Nick's ancestor was Elijah's father? It doesn't really matter. We will honor the possibility no matter what, but in light of the truth," she glanced at Chief Stephenson, "it would be good to know."

I nodded. "DNA will tell you pretty easily. We just need a Benfer descendant to agree to be tested, and Demetrius, you would need to be tested, too, since you are a direct male descendant. The results would tell us quickly if you two are kin. Maybe we could also confirm the Beazley connection while we are looking."

"I don't see Judge Beazley agreeing to a DNA test," Demetrius said. "Sorry."

"Well, we can't know until we ask, can we?" Mika said. "I'll go by his chambers today."

I felt a chill of fear wash over me. I didn't want Mika going anywhere near the Beazleys given Hortense's threat. Santiago must have thought the same thing because he said, "Actually, I'll go. It's official police business at this point."

I breathed a sigh of relief. I wasn't thrilled about Santiago going into harm's way, but I figured he had a better chance of coming out intact than my yarn-selling, super-smart but recklessly curious best friend.

Mika pouted a little, but I thought I might be able to help her perk up. "Feel like taking a trek instead?" I asked.

Her face brightened. "Always ready for an adventure."

"Good, Veronica and Nick, do you mind if we walk around BelAirre today, see what we might find?" I asked.

Veronica nodded. "I can do you one better. We'll drive you around in our Gators. Anyone who wants to wander can come, too."

Mary raised her hand. "I'm in."

"Great," Nick said. "Meet you at the house in fifteen?" After we nodded, he started to walk away but then turned back. "Wait, what are we looking for?

I laughed. "Chimneys, buildings, and most importantly, graves."

"Graves?" Demetrius said. "You think people might be buried out there."

"Oh, people are definitely buried out there," I said. "What I want to know is where and maybe, if we're really lucky, who."

"Why?" Demetrius seemed bothered.

"Because we want to honor their graves, first and foremost," Veronica said. "Right, Paisley?"

"Definitely, but also because if by chance there are marked stones there, they might help us fill in some pieces of this puzzle." I wasn't sure why Demetrius was ruffled, but his attitude made me wary. I glanced over at Santiago, and I could see concern on his face.

Demetrius sighed. "Okay. Sorry. I thought maybe you were going to be digging up graves or something."

My heart sank, and I walked over to my new friend. "Never. Not unless the descendants of those people wanted us to do that. That ground is sacred, and I just want to protect it and try to recover the information we can from those people's final resting place." I reached over and put my hand on his arm. "Sorry to worry you. I should have explained."

He put his hand over mine. "Thank you." He looked over at Veronica. "Mind if I come along, too?"

Veronica nodded. I smiled but then looked down at his fine leather shoes. "Have anything more field-friendly?"

He laughed. "I'm fashionable, not stupid. I'll change inside and meet you over there in a minute. I always keep a change of clothes in the car just in case."

"Be prepared," Santiago said. "Eagle Scout?"

Demetrius grinned. "You know it."

The two men headed toward the church while Mary, Mika, and I piled into the back of the Benfers' car after saying goodbye to Chief Stephenson, who had tribal business to attend to. She asked to be updated if we didn't mind, and I had to resist telling her that if we found anything amazing the whole world would know. Instead, I gave her a hug and told her, "Certainly."

The ride to the Benfers was a treat because I had never ridden in a Tesla before. I couldn't get over how quiet it was or how big the view screen was . . . or how there were no buttons anywhere but on that screen. It felt like cruising in a spaceship, and I loved it.

But when we got to BelAirre, we were all ready to get going, so while Nick and Veronica got the Gators out of the barn, Mika, Mary, and I pulled up some old maps on my phone and started scanning BelAirre for markings.

A friend who specialized in maps had introduced me to the ARC-GIS tool a few months ago, and I was addicted. I could pull up aerial photos of any piece of land from various decades and then overlay them with historic maps to see what had been in a place when. It was like peeling back centuries of development to see how a place had changed. Amazing.

By the time Veronica and Nick got back, we had identified three potential places to look – a grove of trees that was oddly in the middle of a field, a cluster of small buildings at one corner of the property, and a path that went through the woods but seemed to dead-end. When I showed the maps to the Benfers, they marveled a minute and then decided on a fourth place for us to visit, a hill just west of their house that they'd heard might hold another cemetery. They had already preserved one and had just not explored this lead. From the maps, it looked to be still treed, so it was worth a look.

We had our route planned and were ready when Demetrius pulled up, looking distinctly more rugged in jeans and a ratty T-shirt. "You dress down well," I said with a laugh.

"I'll take that as a compliment," he said and climbed in with Nick and Mika.

Then, we took off, and I got a second joyous ride for the day. Veronica clearly knew how to drive the Gator, and she was well-familiar with the roads. So we flew along through the fields, and I reminded myself how much I loved the sensation of wind in my hair and vowed to put my car windows down more often.

When we pulled up to our first stop, the grove of trees, I saw immediately that we weren't going to find a cemetery here. Right in the middle of the grove was a large stream that ran down a steep bank. This spot hadn't been cultivated because it was a drainage from the hill above, not because a cemetery was here.

To be sure, we took a quick walk through the trees but didn't see anything except large oaks. No depressions from graves, no stones, not even any paths to and from the grove. We crossed that one off the list and loaded up to head toward the group of structures we'd seen on the map.

The path to that corner of the property took us along an old fence line that was clear from the cedars that lined it. Then, we reached a small stream, and once we'd forded that water, we came to what were clearly the remains of small buildings. I hopped off and walked around and immediately saw piles of stones, one at each end of the three buildings. "These were houses," I said with confidence and then explained how I knew.

Between the chimney ruins were some standing beams and a lot of decaying wood. I bent down and peered amongst the debris. I could see fragments of turned wood, maybe from chairs or tables, and some colorful glimmers that told me they might be pottery or something. "If you are going to have an archaeologist come out, have them come here," I said.

I pinned this location onto the map and marked it "Quarter" based on my assumption that these were slave quarters, but there wasn't anything here that was going to tell us about the who of the people that lived here. It did, however, tell us a bit about how operations worked.

We stood around my phone, and I showed how back in the early twentieth century, the aerial photos showed the fields around here were planted in corn. "I can't be sure without more research, but I expect the field hands lived here."

"So that they were close to their workplace," Mary said and ran her eyes over the fields. "They would have had to step out the door and go to work. No time to even transition from home to work."

I sighed. Nothing I could say would make this history easier, and it shouldn't be easier. It was horrible in every way, and it was the truth for centuries in our country. I stood silent and thanked the people who had worked here for their labor.

The day was beginning to get really warm, though, and as Nick pointed out, we were moving into prime tick and snake season. So we loaded up and moved to the path we'd spotted that came from near the house out to the top of a ridgeline. There, we found more chimneys, and below, it looked like there was some sort of wall. "Maybe a garden?" I guessed.

Mika took my phone and pulled up the map and went back as far as she could with the aerials. "Looks like it," she said as she passed the image around. "A big one."

I sighed. "So these houses would have been for the folks who gardened and maybe who worked in the barn." I pointed to where we could see the roof of that structure just over the rise.

Demetrius took the phone and then trailed his eyes up the path toward the west. "Is that the hill where you've heard there was a graveyard?" He asked Nick.

"That's it," Nick said. Then, he studied the path at our feet. "Maybe we should walk from here. Just watch where you step."

Solemnly, we followed the trail up the slight slope and into the tree-line. We didn't have to go far before we could all see this was a sacred space. Field stones were lined up in tidy rows with smaller stones about six feet further east. This was clearly a burial ground.

Veronica whispered, "Why didn't we come up here before, Nick? Why didn't we know?"

Nick rubbed her back. "We know now."

Slowly, we all walked in amongst the graves. The crinkle of leaves under our feet filled the silence, and I wondered when someone had visited last. The cemetery was in good shape, at least as far as forgotten places were concerned. There weren't any brambles growing up, and the graves looked undisturbed.

I walked further in, speaking quietly to the people buried there and telling them they were remembered. "You are not forgotten," I said.

"Of course, they're not forgotten," a woman's voice said from the tree-line beyond the graveyard.

Everyone spun and looked at the tall, thin white woman in a long linen skirt who was now walking toward us.

"These are my ancestors. I wouldn't abandon them here." She moved into the cemetery and began placing violet blossoms on each grave. We stood and watched her bend, rest a flower, and speak a few inaudible words at each person's final resting place.

When she was done, she said, "I'm Hortense Beazley. Now, what are you doing on my land?"

I spun to look at Veronica and Nick, but they looked as baffled as I felt. Veronica recovered quickly though and stepped forward. "Hortense, it's nice to finally meet you. I'm Veronica Benfer. I'm afraid there's been some misunderstanding. This is our property."

Hortense straightened her shoulders. "There most certainly has been a misunderstanding, on your part. These are my ancestors, and this is my land. Has been since our," she looked at Nick, "great-great-uncle gave it to my great-grandfather."

Nick walked up. "I'm sorry. I don't understand. Who was your great-great uncle?"

She pointed to a grave right in the corner of the cemetery where a carved stone stood about knee-high, the only carved stone in the cemetery. "His name was Elijah Morris, and he's buried right there."

12

I gasped, and Hortense turned toward me. "You are Elijah's relative?"

She nodded, and then tilted her head. "You know of him?"

I pulled out my phone and opened the family tree I'd made for Elijah's family. "I've been researching his, I mean, your family for Bethel Church." I handed her the phone, and she looked at it briefly.

"So you're the one. Levi said he spoke to you, but you didn't seem willing to listen to reason." Her voice was heavy, sad almost.

"He threatened her," Mika said, "and her son."

My throat was suddenly very tight, and I had to take a deep breath. If I thought things were complicated before. "Yes, that's right. He did," I said softly.

Hortense raised her hands over her head and then let them fall. "I had no idea. I asked him to persuade you to stop your inquiries, but I never sanctioned threats. I do apologize." She turned to Nick again. "Your brother does have a quick temper."

Nick nodded, but from the puzzled looked on his face, I

could tell he was as lost as I was. Still, we were on the trail of good information, and I wasn't about to let that go.

"Ms. Beazley, I'm Paisley Sutton. The Benfers," I gestured over to them, "hired me to help research the people who were enslaved at BelAirre. If I am understanding you correctly, then you are a descendant of those people. Is that right?"

"It is," she said, "even though I don't look like most people imagine I would." She scanned her eyes over each of us. "Perhaps we should all sit down, have a glass of sweet tea, and talk." She turned and then looked back at us. "My house is just over this way."

In a silent procession, we followed her down the hill to where, just below, her beautiful farmhouse sat. I'd never noticed it before, tucked as it was behind the hill from the road, but it was lovely. Simple and understated with a wide front porch lined with prolific pink peonies. BelAirre was beautiful, but this house felt comfortable, lived in.

She led us to the porch and suggested we all sit in the wicker seats and rocking chairs there while she got tea. I offered to help, but she said, "I so rarely have company. Let me wait on you, please."

We all sat down and enjoyed the lovely view into the valley below. Fields and fence lines snaked across the scene, and I could see how I might never leave this house if this was the peaceful view I had.

A few moments later, Hortense returned with a tray and seven tall glasses of tea that were already beading up with condensation in the rising heat of the day. We each took one and quietly sipped the sweet liquid while we waited for someone to speak.

I finally broke the silence by saying, "Hortense, forgive me for being so forward, but we are trying to figure out some things related to the church and your great-great- Uncle Elijah.

Do you mind it I ask you to tell me about your family line?" I smiled and hoped my question wasn't too intrusive.

"Of course," she said, "but first, can you tell me what you know? Forgive me, but I am a very private person, and while I think you are sincere with your motives, you can imagine that my family has not always been treated well given our lineage." She sat back and held me in her gaze.

"Definitely," I said. "I'm sorry. I should have begun there." I told her the full story of the week, of how we had found Earnestine Greene's journals and then confirmed there was a Monacan burial ground under the church's manse. I explained how our research also led us to think Earnestine had been murdered for trying to stop the building of the manse and then how further inquiry had led us to understand that the Benfers and Beazleys were related through Nicholas the Fourth and Anne.

"You have done a lot of work, and it all seems accurate as best I know. I'd be glad to help if I can." She paused. "But first, let me answer your question. I am Emily Morris's great-granddaughter."

I sucked in a breath. "She was Elijah's sister," I said quietly.

"Correct. She came here as an infant and was given the Beazley name, then raised here, first as a slave and then as a housemaid after she was freed at the end of The War." She sipped her tea again. "After moving into town and taking a place as a white woman, she was very light-skinned, she married a white man, Thomas Shepherd, from Charlottesville. They lived there and raised their children, who kept the Beazley name, but then Elijah bought the land from the Beazleys and gave it to my great-grandmother, his sister, because it was easier for her and her husband to be landowners of this scale than it was for him."

"And then the land passed from her to your grandfather and so on," Nick said.

"Correct. One small sleight of hand to bely the firmness of racial categories, and here we are." She swallowed. "You can see why I was concerned that people were exploring this history."

I nodded. "You were worried that someone might try to take the land away, that somehow your claim would be undermined."

She sighed. "I was. I am. See, I don't know how Elijah came to hold title to this property. Nothing in our family record explains that, and so . . ." Her voice trailed off.

"You are worried that he got it illegally," Demetrius said as he leaned forward. "You need not worry. Our ancestor was law-abiding and generous."

"Our ancestor," Hortense said and put her hand to her lips. "We are related."

Demetrius smiled. "Cousins," He said. "I am Demetrius Cleveland, a descendant of Elisa Mae Morris, Elijah's grand-daughter." He stood and shook her hand. "It's nice to meet you."

A tear slid down Hortense's cheek. "I'm so glad to know you," she said. "I was under the impression that my uncle was the only other kin I had, and he is not interested – no, he's downright disdainful of our family story, 'the legend of Elijah,' he calls it."

I smiled. "Oh, it's not legend. Your Elijah Morris was a wealthy man, and we can prove it. He bought this land clear and free; I have no doubt. This is your land, Hortense. Your family's land." I felt tears welling up in my eyes as I spoke.

Hortense looked at me, "Really?"

Mika sat forward and explained what Mrs. Stephenson had found in the ledgers. "Given circumstances, I expect Elijah did his best to keep his wealth quiet, but he definitely had it," Mika finished, "which means he bought this land, built this house, with his own money. It's rightfully yours."

"What is rightfully yours?" Levi Benfer stomped up the

porch steps and stood behind Hortense. "What's going on here?"

"Levi, meet my cousin Demetrius," Hortense said.

Demetrius stood and put out his hand to shake Levi's. Levi just stared.

"Levi Benfer, shame on you," Veronica said. "We met Hortense at the cemetery on the top of the hill, and we've been making connections between our family and hers."

The color drained from Levi's face. "So you know?" he said to Hortense. "I guess I should have realized you would find out."

"Find out what, Levi?" Her face was etched deep with worry.

"That you and I are cousins." He sighed.

Hortense furrowed her brow and then looked over at me. "Are we cousins? Is that right?"

"Technically yes, but so far back that it doesn't matter in any way except that your family tree will become simpler a few generations back." I was puzzled by Levi's reaction. "Is that what was worrying you? That if Hortense found out you two were related, she might end your relationship."

A flush spread up Levi's neck, and then he nodded almost imperceptibly.

"Oh my goodness, you ridiculous man. Why would any such thing matter? Everyone is related to everyone somehow, and here in Octonia, well, most of us are probably married to our kin," Hortense said with a laugh. Then, she leaned over and gave Levi a deep, lingering kiss.

The blush crowned the top of Levi's head beneath his blonde hair as he pulled away. "I guess I am a little ridiculous, but I didn't want to lose you," he said.

Mary sighed deeply, and I grinned at her. She was a dyed-in-the-wool romantic if ever there was one. Given the fact that I was a little teary again, I guess I was, too.

Hortense and Levi looked like they needed a minute to discuss. The confusion and concern on Nick and Veronica's faces told me they might be eager to have some family conversations. Demetrius was sitting quietly, but I could see Veronica's hand on his arm. He was ready for some good family chatting, too.

So the rest of us said our goodbyes and headed back up the hill to the Gators after Levi assured us that he would get Nick and Veronica home. As I walked away, I glanced back and thought, *This is what it should have looked like all along. The whole family, black and white, on that porch together.*

But as we crested the hill and walked quietly through the cemetery again, I couldn't help but think about how many people had spent so much energy trying very hard not to let that small reunion happen. Something tingled down my spine, and I took a deep breath. One mystery was solved, but this was far from over.

Once we had parked the Gators and headed back to town, I checked in with Lucille only to hear that Sawyer was in their backyard, buck naked and playing in the sprinkler. "We'll feed him lunch and then bring him over with the hopes he falls asleep on the way. Keep you posted," she replied.

I grinned. Even with the nap, that boy would be ready for bed early given all this excitement. And I was glad for some more work time.

As Mika and I walked into the shop, I saw Mrs. Stephenson helping a young woman pick out some baby yarn in a beautiful green, and I grinned. If I could, I'd probably have an entire wardrobe made from that soft, sweet yarn. It felt so good against my skin.

When the purchase was completed, Mrs. Stephenson joined us in the Cozy Corner, and we caught her up on the morning's events. She actually clapped in delight at the news and said, "I've pulled together all the figures in a spreadsheet with references to the ledgers, so while it's not proof until we find evidence that Elijah actually had the money, it is pretty clear."

"Well, that's my next stop. I'm going back to the courthouse to try and pull all the land records under Elijah's name together. It won't show us his cash, but if he had property that he purchased, he had to acquire it somehow," I said.

"Good plan," Mika said and then looked at Mrs. Stephenson, "Mind showing me that spreadsheet, while we have a lull?"

I picked up my bag as Mrs. Stephenson trotted over to get her laptop and told Mika I'd be back ASAP, hopefully before Sawyer. "Oh, don't worry if you're not," Mrs. Stephenson said, "I have a spider-related craft for us to do."

I smiled and decided to take my time then, even as I thought about how grateful I was that Sawyer and I had such a great group of people to care for us.

At the clerk's office, I pulled the appropriate deed index and turned to the page where Elijah Morris was listed. Then, I gasped and pulled out my phone. He had almost an entire column of records in his name. The man had bought and sold a lot of land in his lifetime. I felt my pulse quicken as I got closer to the proof we were all hoping to find.

As I began to pull out the deed books and photograph the various land purchases that Morris had executed, I started to dance around in excitement, and the other researchers in the room gave me shy smiles and laughs until one brave man said, "Okay, what has you so excited?"

For a minute I didn't answer as I weighed the reward-to-risk ratio in my head. But then, I realized that this news was going to be out sooner rather than later, and I might as well see what these land title experts could do to help. So I said, "I've just discovered an enslaved man inherited a lot of money from his enslaver and then used much of that cash to buy land around Octonia."

I gestured toward the deed index. "He has almost a whole column of listings here, and now I'm tracking down the deeds."

The man stood up. "Want some help?"

I grinned. "Absolutely." As I watched, four other people stood from their computer terminals and came over. I divvied out the references to the deed books, and in a minute, all six of us had deed books open and cameras out.

The room soon filled with chatter as we read out names and dates and began to assemble a timeline of Elijah's land purchases. He did occasionally sell a parcel, but for the most part, he bought lots of smaller acreage all around the town of Octonia.

An hour later, we had assembled a full list of his land holdings, and when we added the acreage, we found he owned over 1,480 acres of land, all in small parcels scattered around town. That was a huge chunk of property for anyone to own, but for a black man to have that kind of land holding in the early twentieth century was, as far as I knew, one of a kind for our rural county.

But we didn't stop there, we then began looking at the chain of title for each of those parcels, and my new research assistants soon made quick work of that process since this was their bread and butter as title researchers. They followed the ownership of each parcel right up to today, and recorded every owner on a separate sheet of paper for each piece of land.

This process was slower and more tedious than just looking up the deeds, and it would have taken me days to accomplish what these five people finished in two hours. When they handed me their records, I could quickly see that Elijah's land has become the property of many African American families in Octonia, and I knew that most of those families would be excited to know this bit of history.

But there were three parcels that were puzzling because, as best as we could all tell, they had never been sold. One was

Hortense's property of almost a hundred acres. The other was a five-acre plot at the back of the Bethel Church land, and I knew that parcel deserved a little further investigating. But the third piece really caught my eye because it was right at the edge of town, in almost exactly the spot that developers had been talking about putting a big box store.

Fortunately, one of the title researchers had been working on that real estate transaction and had already pulled the title records from the supposed purchase. She hadn't yet done the search for all the parcels, and when she saw this one, she squeaked. "This property doesn't have a clear title." She cleared her throat. "Or rather it does, but it's not owned by the people who claimed to have owned it."

She showed me the last known deed for that eight-acre parcel, and I saw there, clear as day, Elijah Morris's name. "So he and his heirs still own this property?" I said.

"Right, but they need to act fast. It's about to become a drive-thru in the new shopping center," the woman said.

I sat down heavily at one of the wooden chairs. Just when we were making headway in clearing up all these historical land issues, we find a new one. I felt overwhelmed with what this might mean.

"Don't worry," the woman said as she put her phone to her ear and sat down beside me. "This is what I do. I'm calling the agent who brokered the sale now. We have some time."

For the next few minutes, I listened to her explain to the real estate broker what she had found, and I could hear the strain in the man's voice on the other end. But when my new friend hung up, she said, "The sale now has to be reviewed. I can't tell you anything about the buyer, but your friends, Elijah Morris's descendants, have a clear case to halt the sale or to demand compensation for their land."

I was already texting Veronica and Nick, but the researcher put her hand on mine. "They really have to act fast. If they don't file a claim, the courts can push the sale through by seizing the land for back taxes."

I sighed. "They won't let that happen." I sent off my text and packed up my bag with a huge word of thanks to my five new assistants. "You are all the best. Do you mind if I thank you publicly in my newsletter?"

The woman who had just called the broker said, "Maybe just call us your Research Angels. It might be better if folks didn't know who we were."

I nodded. "Got it. Your secret is safe with me," I said as I headed toward the door. "Now, if you'll excuse me, I have an illegal land purchase to help stop."

The small group applauded as I headed out the door, and I left the courthouse feeling both hopeful and terrified. It was, sadly, a familiar feeling.

When I got back to Mika's store, Sawyer was wrapping the entire back-third of the shop in yarn, but rather than just a haphazard pattern, Mrs. Stephenson had him making a pattern of concentric rings that looked, perfectly, like a spider web. Each time he started to go a little wild with the pattern, she gently guided him back to his purpose, to catch a giant spider.

From the look on his face, I could tell he was working really hard, and when I kissed him on the top of his head, he barely looked up. I shot Mrs. Stephenson a grateful smile and sat down at my makeshift desk.

I'd asked Hortense, Veronica, and Nick to stop by if they could, and I needed to pull my thoughts and notes together to talk with them about next steps. The title researcher had given me the broker's name, so I knew that their first step was to call him and get together the proof that they held claim to the title. Given that the judge was Hortense's uncle, I was hoping that maybe she could appeal to him directly too.

By the time my friends arrived, I had produced three print-outs, thanks to the use of Mika's printer, with all the information they needed, including copies of the deed and the notes about how there were no further deeds, the broker's name, and the exact plat number in the county land records. I explained to all three of them the situation, and then I sent them to work.

I had wanted to give them the exciting news about all of Elijah's land holdings back in the day, but time was of the essence, and I didn't want to slow them down.

FORTUNATELY, I didn't have long to brood as I waited to hear what my friends were doing about the land because Santiago came in soon after they left, and the long face he wore told me that his trip to ask Judge Beazley about a DNA test had not gone well. "He flat out refused. Said that was all ancient history and those DNA tests could be rigged. He then went on to threaten me with removal from my position if I continued to push this ridiculousness or 'dig up' – his exact words – trouble at the church. 'Let the past be," he said before kicking me out of his chambers."

I blew air out of my lips and groaned. "Well, I don't suppose Hortense is going to have much more luck about the land then."

"What land?" Santiago asked, and I got him up to speed on what the research team had found that afternoon.

Santiago leaned back in the folding chair next to me and said, 'Well, if it means he might have claim to the land, too . . ."

I stared at him. "Oh, I didn't even think of that. He might stop the sale then."

"Or he might let it go through but with a huge price tag." Santiago said with a sad smile. "I get the impression that His Honor is sort of all about his own power and influence."

I let my head fall back and stared at the ceiling. "Well, at least we have informed the proper people, and they can make the best decision for their family." I sighed. "Now, I really need to figure out what all this means for Earnestine Greene and the church." I was back to where I started, and while the adventure into a broader scope had been fun, I knew I needed to focus my attention on what brought me into all of this to begin with.

"Well, about that, I did speak with Chief Stephenson today, and she and the Tribal Council are beginning the archaeological research tomorrow. They invited the two of us and Mary to be on site. Can you go?" I looked over at Sawyer and smiled. "Do you think they'd mind a three-year-old's presence?" I hadn't been with my boy much this week, and I missed him. I wanted to spend a day with him before he went to his dad's for the weekend.

"The chief expressly invited him; told me he could work with her as they watch the archaeologists." He smiled.

"Perfect. Although I don't know how patient he's going to be with archaeological methods." I was imagining all the movies and shows I'd seen with brushes and millimeters of dirt removal.

"All taken care of. Saul is bringing in trucks of fill dirt for when the site needs to be sealed again, so Sawyer can dig as much as he wants there."

I laughed. "I'll pick up extra bubble bath on the way home then."

"How about I treat you and Sawyer to tacos and then we hit the grocery store together?" Santiago said with a grin. "Maybe between the two of us we can keep him from pulling everything off the shelves."

I'd told Santiago about the challenges of grocery shopping with the most curious child on the planet, so I was thrilled to hear his offer. Behind me, I heard a squeal and turned just in time to see Mrs. Stephenson bring out a giant crocheted spider for Sawyer's new web.

"It's enormous," Sawyer said as he tried out one of his new words. "Can I hug it?

"Of course you can," Mrs. Stephenson said. "Her name is Charlotte, and I thought maybe you and I could read a book about her when you come here with your mom."

I grinned. *Charlotte's Web* was one of my favorite books of all time, and I knew that Sawyer would love it if he could sit still long enough to listen. Somehow, I thought this set-up and the promise of time with Mrs. Stephenson might just be the magic combo to get him to settle for reading.

Meanwhile, Mika was snapping photos of the giant web and spider. "I'm going to sell kits for this exact thing," she said to me as she tapped away on Instagram. "Thank you!," she said to Mrs. Stephenson.

"Oh, that's a great idea, dear," the older woman said. "I'll help you assemble the kits."

I looked over at my son, and I could see the day catching up with him as he started to get clumsy and slow down. "I predict we have one hour before melt-down," I said to Santiago. "Maybe grocery store and then tacos to go?"

"You got it," He said as he scooped Sawyer up over his shoulder. "Let's go get you some cereal, Little Man," he said.

Sawyer laughed and kicked as we waved goodbye.

THE GROCERY STORE run turned into a laugh-fest as Santiago clowned around with Sawyer as I tried to grab everything we might need as quickly as we could. Despite my best efforts, we did end up with a tray of cream horns and a gigantic bag of lime tortilla chips. But we also got some milk, some mushrooms, the much-needed bubble bath, and a variety of healthy food options for the house.

By the time we were in the car with tacos on the way home, Sawyer looked ready to drop off any minute, so Santiago drove, and I sat in the back to tickle my son awake as needed. Then we ate, did a sponge bath with wipes, and headed to bed. I spent a few minutes snuggling my little boy and realizing just how much I'd missed him. I told him how proud I was of him for being with Baba and Boppy overnight, and then I held him close as he drifted off.

Back downstairs, Santiago had brewed us raspberry tea, and we went out to the porch to watch the fireflies and listen to the frogs.

Throughout the evening, we'd each gotten calls about the situation in which we found ourselves embroiled, but it didn't look like much was going ahead tonight. Veronica said Judge Beazley had expressed great interest in the land deal but that it sounded like he was happy to sell and, if he could finagle it, keep the proceeds himself. She didn't mind that except that she wished Hortense and Demetrius could get their fair share as his other heirs. That was tomorrow's project, she said. "Operation Split the Money," she said with a laugh that sounded equal parts hopeful and sad.

Mary texted to say she was eager to see me in the morning, that she thought she'd found something in the church records that might be a clue and would show it to me in the morning.

And Santiago talked to Savannah, who was busy securing the burial site at the church for tomorrow's endeavors. So far, she'd had to send several amateur filmmakers and three members of the Board of Supervisors away, so Santiago called in a few officers from nearby Madison County to work security overnight and through tomorrow. "It's not my favorite thing to use our limited funds on since people should simply be respectful of burial grounds, but it is what it is," he said as he turned off the sound on his phone, tucked it into his shirt pocket, and turned to me. "But now, how are you?"

"I was going to ask you the same thing." I sat back and stretched out my legs. "I'm thrilled we're finding so much information, but I also feel really sad that all this remained hidden for so long."

He nodded. "And to think it's only that you happened to find journals from a woman dead almost a hundred years that brought all this to light."

I winced and gave thanks that Mary and I had thought to check the house one more time. "But we're no closer to finding out what happened to Earnestine," I said, letting that disappointment really sink in. "Maybe what Mary found will help."

Santiago took my hand. "Maybe it will, and I'll keep investigating too. I have a feeling we're not far off from answers, Paisley. Just keep looking."

I nodded and then lifted his hand to my lips to kiss his knuckles before settling back to let the silence soothe us both.

A little while later after the summer quiet had settled me a bit, I sat up and said, "Feel like watching a little TV, keep me company while I sew?"

"I'd like that. *Ozark*?" My law-enforcement boyfriend loved this dark and gritty show about a family who gets involved with gangsters and has to do horrible things to protect their own. I loved Jason Bateman, the lead, so I was always happy to watch.

Unfortunately, we had only started the show when my phone rang. It was Savannah, and she needed to speak with Santiago immediately. I passed him the phone, paused the TV, and put my cross-stitch dump truck back in my basket as I watched Santiago's face, which had grown drawn and gray as he listened. "I'll be there in five minutes. I'm in Paisley's car." He glanced at me as I nodded. His car was still downtown, and he and I had talked about him driving mine home and then coming to get Sawyer and me for the dig in the morning.

"Everything okay?" I asked while knowing it clearly wasn't.

"A mob of people led by Levi Benfer has gathered at the church. I need to get down there." He was already halfway to the door. "I'll call you later." He waved and then rushed out after grabbing my keys from the counter.

I texted Mary and Mika to let them know what was going

on, and I thought about calling Chief Stephenson then decided that was better handled by Santiago when he could give her more information. My call would just worry her without a lot of detail.

Mika and Mary responded immediately, and as I sewed and watched *Blown Away*, a reality show about glass blowers that had no plot and only interesting art, I tried to keep myself from worrying, too. It had seemed like Levi had been okay today when he'd learned that Hortense wasn't in danger from what we'd been finding. But clearly something else had happened, or he had been a very good actor.

Either way, the situation was ugly, and I suddenly wasn't looking forward to our visit to the church in the morning. I could only hope Santiago could quell tempers before someone did something stupid.

I STAYED up way too late waiting to hear from Santiago, but I also finished Sawyer's dump truck in the process. So I was buoyed by accomplishment even if I was exhausted when my son tapped my cheek and said, "Time to get up" at seven-fifteen a.m..

Santiago had let me know that the situation had been resolved the night before, and he was planning to come get us at eight so that he could be on site to relieve the night watch. I hustled Sawyer into clothes and then through breakfast – waffles with honey, one of his favorites – and then I slipped into my most comfy presentable jeans and T-shirt and gathered our snacks for the day.

When Santiago pulled in, Saw bounded up the driveway to meet him while Beauregard followed along. Sometimes that cat really did think he was a dog. Fortunately, Beau got bored and headed back inside pretty quickly, which made strapping Sawyer into his seat and shutting up the house much simpler. I could tell Santiago was eager to get to the site, and I didn't want to hold him up.

As soon as we arrived, he stepped out with a smile at me and headed toward where Savannah stood looking vigilant but also weary. All around the edge of the property I could see men in black cargo pants and polos standing with their eyes facing out. They were ready for an arrival from any direction. This sight might have put me at ease, but instead, I just felt more anxious.

Just as promised, there was a very large pile of dirt just beyond the edge of the trees in front of the dig site, and Sawyer didn't waste one minute heading there, tiny plastic trowel and bucket in hand. Somehow, I thought this activity might be even more fun for him than building the sandcastles that his tools were designed for.

With my son occupied, I decided to spend a few minutes reviewing my notes and staying out of Santiago's way. He would tell me what I needed to know later, but for now, it looked like he had his hands full briefing the van of new security guards who had just arrived. I really had never seen so much muscle clad in black in my life.

I sat down in one of the chairs beneath the trees so I could see Sawyer but also enjoy the shade in the cool-ish morning. Then, I took out the notebook where I'd been recording my thoughts about Earnestine Greene and read through them.

Then, I turned to a blank page and wrote down what I knew:

1. She had known about the burial ground, it seemed, from the time the parish house was built or soon thereafter.
2. She had wrestled with who to tell and when and had decided to tell on the day when more damage could be done with the new addition to the manse.

3. She had died on the same day she recorded her decision to tell the deacon board.

4. Her cause of death was listed as an accidental fall down the stairs.

5. Demetrius Cleveland's grandfather had been the informant on the death certificate.

6. Demetrius Cleveland was related to Elijah Morris.

I paused and stared into space. That last note made something fire in my brain, and I had to stop and let the synapses get the information to where I could grab it. I waited and stared as I let the ideas bounce around, and then I had it.

If Demetrius was related to Elijah so were the Benfers, all three of them, and Hortense Beazley, too. He was the progenitor of their family line, and as such, all of them had something to gain – or maybe lose – from that information.

I flipped open my laptop, connected to my phone's hotspot, and followed my genealogical instinct. Within a matter of minutes, I could see that all of those people – the Benfer men, Demetrius Cleveland, and Hortense Beazley – had relatives living in this area at the time Earnestine Greene was killed.

My heart was racing. I didn't want to think about that, but it seemed that any one of my new friends could have good reason for wanting to stop my queries.

The part I couldn't figure out, still, was how the Monacan burial ground mattered to anyone now. Levi Benfer sure seemed to care, though. I just could not figure out why.

As I watched three cars pull into the parking lot, I decided to let my subconscious work on that question, and I rose to greet Chief Stephenson. She said hello and asked how I was doing, and then she headed straight for Sawyer, who was already tinted brown from the dirt and currently digging a hole to the center of the pile. When Chief Stephenson called to him, though, he popped his dirty head out of the hole and said, "Hello."

She stepped up the hill to him, and when she leaned over and whispered in his ear, he jumped up and then raced down the pile and full speed. The phrase "Jack came tumbling after" whizzed through my head as I stepped in front of him to keep him from careening into the chairs around me. "Slow down, Little Man," I said. "Where you off to so fast?"

"Chief Stephenson said I could dig the first shovelful in the giant hole." I looked over at the woman who had walked back over to join us.

"That's very generous of you," I said.

"It's our pleasure. This way, Sawyer will know about our history and our present, and maybe he'll be a part of helping us preserve our stories, just like his mama." She squeezed my arm before taking Sawyer's hand and leading him to the small group of people standing beside the space where the basement had been.

I trailed behind, eager to hear what was being said but careful not to intrude. The archaeologist in charge of today's dig was setting out the parameters. "We're not trying to excavate anything more than the bare minimum here. We're not removing anything beyond what we need to confirm this is a burial site. So if you see anything, please photograph it and then call me or my assistant here to record the location. Then, the Chief and the council can decide whether to remove it or leave it be. Understood?"

I looked at the group of about ten people surrounding him. Including Chief Stephenson and two of the members of the Tribal Council I'd met before, the group included two Boy Scouts, probably here to earn their Eagle Scout rank, the two archaeologists, and three others I had never seen. As the group headed toward the pit, Chief Stephenson introduced me to the three younger people I didn't know, all were members of the

Monacan Nation enrolled in a summer class about tribal history. They were clearly very excited to be included today. Mary and Demetrius also stood nearby, but, like me, were here only to observe, not dig.

Chief Stephenson took Sawyer by the hand and then carefully lowered him into one of the Boy Scout's arms below. Then, she climbed down the ladder next to him. As I stood above and watched, she thanked the ancestors for bringing them here today and asked for guidance in their work.

Then, she turned to Sawyer, pointed to his shovel, and said, "You first, Sawyer. Where do we begin?"

My son tapped his cheek in thought and then pointed toward a small indentation near the center of the hole. "There," he said, and walked confidently toward his chosen spot. Then, after getting a nod from Chief Stephenson, he plunged his red shovel into the dirt and slowly lifted a pile of earth into the air before carefully pouring it out on a tarp the archaeologists had laid out.

"Now, Little Guy, we need to look through this dirt very carefully to see if we find anything,' the head archaeologist said.

Saw nodded solemnly and then knelt down by his shovel of dirt. He put his hands into the drying earth and began to break it up with his tiny fingers. Within seconds, he said, "Is this what we are looking for?"

He held up a small patch of fabric that was stiff with dirt. When Sawyer brushed his fingers over the top, the dirt fell away and revealed a swirling flower of blue beadwork. The entire site went silent, and I let the tears stream down my face. My son had found just what we hoped – evidence of Monacan presence here.

Chief Stephenson knelt down next to Saw and took hold of the other side of the piece he held. "Yes, Sawyer. Just like this. One of my ancestors made this. They sewed it by hand and wore it on special occasions. Thank you for finding it for us. We had lost it, but now, we have found it. We have found them." She pulled Sawyer to her and gave him a gentle hug.

When she glanced up at me, I smiled. Then, as Sawyer handed her the piece of what was now clearly identifiable as beaded leather, I climbed down, hugged my son, and suggested he go see what else he could find in the big pile of dirt.

As he and I climbed back out, I looked down and saw Chief Stephenson examining the piece Sawyer had found. She held it in the palm of her hand and studied it. Then, after the archaeologist photographed it and placed a flag to mark its location, the chief returned it to the ground, to the person with whom it had been buried.

Sawyer dug for an hour or so longer while the team in the pit checked a few more sites to confirm that Sawyer's find was not just a fluke. But soon they had not only recovered several more pieces of clothing, but they had also unearthed human remains. There was no doubt this was a Monacan burial site, and with that confirmation, the team withdrew, Saul arrived with his backhoe, picked up Sawyer and put him in the cab with him and the two of them carefully and gently refilled the pit.

There wouldn't be a press release or any public statement because, as we'd all learned, these sites were sacred and endangered. Ms. Dixon from the Department of Historic Resources came by and gathered the documentation to officially register the site, but it would not even be formally mapped on any public record. The presence of these people's remains would be protected, but not publicized. Somehow that seemed just perfect.

When Sawyer and Saul finished filling the site, everyone except Mary, Santiago, Sawyer, Saul, and I headed home. It has been a momentous morning, and with all the events of the week pressing down on us, everyone was due for a long nap and a relaxing night.

But before Saul left, Mary wondered if he could ask one more favor. She looked over at me. "I took the plat behind the church that you photographed for me to the courthouse early, and then a friend who is a surveyor came out while you all were digging and checked the metes and bounds."

"Is the property the church's?" I asked.

She shook her head. "No, it technically belongs to Hortense Beazley, but she's just started proceedings to sell it to the church for a dollar. And she gave permission, in writing, for us to begin siting the addition for the church there."

I smiled. "That's great news."

"Sure is," Saul said. "How can I help?"

"I'd like to give our members a way to visualize the addition when they come on Sunday. We're all distraught over the fact that we built on a burial group, and I want to assure everyone we are not violating anyone's final rest to build out back." Mary pointed toward the wooded grove directly behind the building. "Would you mind clearing a few of those trees?"

"Sure. Just point me to what you want," Saul said. "Sawyer, want to help?"

As if Saul needed to ask.

WITHIN A FEW MINUTES, the bulldozer has cleared the first row of trees and was making short work of the understory beneath. Sawyer was laughing and squealing as Saul let him lower the bucket into a thicket of brambles. When they ripped out of the ground, his shout of celebration probably reached the other side of town.

As they worked, I turned back to my own research, determined that I could find something new, something that would clarify everything. But I just kept coming up with documents that confirmed what I already knew. Good for certainty, bad for discovery.

Fortunately, Mary joined me just as I started to get frustrated, and when she sat down, her chair bounced with her excitement. "You aren't going to believe this, Paisley?" she said as she handed me a folder full of papers.

In the excitement of the morning, I had completely forgotten that she had something to show me, but when I opened the folder, I almost fell out of my seat. The photograph showed a tall, thin black woman with perfectly styled hair and an ankle-length dress standing behind the church that I was sitting beside. At the bottom, someone had penned, "Earnestine Greene, pastor's wife."

I looked up at Mary. "This is her," I said quietly. "Wow. She's gorgeous. Stately."

Mary nodded. "She is, but it's her body language I want you to consider."

I looked back at the photo. She was standing straight up with her right hand on her hip, but her left hand was held up and out, like she was carrying a tray. At first, I thought she was simply striking a fun pose for the photo, but then I noticed her index finger was extended while the rest were folded into her palm. "She's pointing at something," I shouted.

Mary stood up and walked toward the church as I followed. Then, she took up the exact position and posture that Earnestine had in the photo, and instantly, I could see she was gesturing into the woods behind the church. The woods that Mary had just requested be cleared.

My mouth dropped open, and I started to say, "You sneaky wo—" when Saul gave a shout.

Mary and I exchanged a brief look of surprise and then jogged into the woods, where we could just see the glimmer of the yellow machine. When we reached them, we stopped short and stared. There, almost entirely covered in honeysuckle vines, was a shack. It was made of graying wood, and if I had come across it in any other situation, I would have assumed it was a little hunter's cabin that was used to keep warm in the late autumn deer season.

But given what we knew and the photo of Earnestine that Mary had just shared, I knew that wasn't any hunter's shack. She and I both lunged toward the building, but just before we began to tug vines off the walls, Saul grabbed us both by the shoulders. "Ladies, there's poison ivy all through there. Let me. I'm not allergic."

I stepped back quickly — as allergic as I was I could get the stuff by seeing it – and stepped up onto the track of the bull-dozer where Sawyer was watching intently. "We found a building, Mama," he said.

I pulled him close and said, "You did a good job, Little Man. When we get inside, we may find what we need, too. Thank you."

He smiled but never took his eyes off Saul, who was making quick work of the vines around the door. Mary was standing quietly nearby, the folder with Earnestine's photo held tightly in her hands. I could see the other pieces of paper behind the photo. "What else is in that folder?"

She looked up at me. "More information about Earnestine from the church files. Most of it talks about how she loved history, was always looking into the family trees of church members, seeing if she could find out more about their families . She was the church historian, it seems."

I nodded. "That explains a lot, right?" Clearly this woman knew a lot more than the average church member, and I feared we were about to learn just what had gotten her killed.

"Okay, if you go carefully, you can get in. The building looks solid, but I wouldn't go wrestling and bumping against the walls now, ladies." Saul grinned.

"No WWE moves," Mary said. "Got it." Then, she slid

through the door Saul had shoved open with me close behind her.

Inside, we both gasped. It was a study, Earnestine's study. The walls were lined with bookshelves and a table with an oil lamp sat next to a sheaf of paper. Mary moved around the table and studied the pages. "They're too faded to read in this light, but it looks like a family tree, maybe."

I stared over her shoulder, and I could just make out the branching shape of words in pairs of two, but like Mary, I couldn't read it.

We moved onto the shelves and studied the spines of the leather volumes there. Each had a single word on it – "Canaan," "Shifflett," "Bonham," "Morris." These are family genealogy books, I knew it. Those names were Octonia names going way back. "This was Earnestine's research space," I whispered.

Mary sighed and took the Morris volume off the shelf. She turned and set it on the table, and as soon as she opened the pages, the scent of paper and ink wafted through the air. I breathed deeply and lifted up a word of thanks to Earnestine. Here, we may have answers.

13

As carefully as we could, we loaded our arms with books and walked back out into the forest around the shack. "We need something to transport a lot of books," I told Saul.

He looked at me, nodded, and took out his phone. "Hey. You at the lot. Bring the front-end loader over to the church site. Keep it quiet, will you?"

I smiled. "Thanks. We don't know what we have here, yet, so yeah, thanks."

Sawyer came over and touched the books stacked in my arms. "What are these, Mama?

I set the stack of books in the cab of Saul's bulldozer and said, "These are books about a lot of the families around here. At least we think they are."

"Is there a book about our family?" he said.

"I don't know yet, Saul, but probably not. Most of these seem to be about the people who went to church here." I knew this was a lot for him to understand, but I believed in telling him the truth, even if it was hard or confusing.

"But you go to church here." he said with a furrowed brow.

"Let me see if I can find our book." He jogged past me and went into the building.

With a smile at Mary, I followed my son into this repository of genealogy and stood in awe again. There must have been two hundred volumes on those shelves, and I couldn't imagine the number of hours she had put into all this work.

With deep concentration, Sawyer was looking at each of the books and "reading" the names on the spine. "O-o-cookie." "Kakaluna." "Sankatoto." Recently, he'd begun pretending to read by using made-up words. It made my heart skip with delight, and now I just felt absolutely overwhelmed with joy.

But there was a shadow of sorrow here, too because for some reason she had needed to hide what she was doing. Otherwise why not work at home or even in the church library? Clearly, she didn't want most people to know she had this vast collection of information, and now we had another mystery to solve.

Plus, I couldn't help wondering who had built this shack for her. I had no doubt she was capable, but I imagined that the sight of a woman, especially a pastor's wife, buying lumber and nails might have stirred up some gossip. No, a man had to construct this for her, and for some reason, I didn't think her husband, the pastor, had done it.

Once Sawyer was sure there wasn't a Sutton volume on the shelves, we went back out, loaded the books we could carry into our arms and tromped back out to the parking lot, where we quickly deposited all the volumes in my car and Mary's. No need for someone to see what we had found before we were ready to talk about it. I figured if Earnestine had felt the need to keep things secret, we needed to honor that until we knew more. Mary seemed to agree.

The only person paying us any attention was Santiago, who had been in his cruiser managing paperwork and answering phone calls while Saul worked. Now, though, he was headed toward our cars with a very puzzled look on his face.

"Anything I should know about?" he asked as he looked from me to Mary.

"Definitely," I said, "but let's sit down." The three of us returned to the circle of chairs while Saul and Sawyer went back into the woods to retrieve the bulldozer.

Mary showed him the folder with Earnestine's picture and the various articles and bulletins about her historical research. "But that's just the tip of the iceberg." She then explained what we found in the shack and what we thought all the books were.

Santiago stared at Earnestine's photo for a few moments after Mary finished speaking, and then he said, "So you think these books may tell us who killed her?"

I nodded. "I think it may not have been the fact that she told the deacons about the burial ground at all." The idea had been worming its way through my synapses for days now, ever since Levi Benfer had tried to put a stop to my research. But only now was the thought coming together. "I think she found out a family secret that someone really didn't want told."

Mary huffed. "I was thinking the same thing. I hate secrets," she said quietly.

"Me, too, " I added. "Me, too."

Just then Saul's guy with the front end loader pulled up, and while he and Saul unloaded one machine and reloaded the bulldozer, I asked Santiago, "So do we have your permission to take these books and study them?" I didn't want to disturb a crime scene or something, and I definitely wanted official permission to take the books.

"Definitely, but I will need to be there. Just for the sake of any court case, okay?" He looked from me to Mary, and we both nodded. "Your house?"

Mary smiled. "Perfect. I'll just swing home for the lasagna I prepped for tonight."

I laughed. "I love you," I said and gave her a big hug.

It only took a few minutes to get all the books into the bucket of the front end loader and then transfer them to our cars. Then, we got into our vehicles and made our way to my house, Mary by way of lasagna and Santiago by way of the station where he let the dispatcher know where he was and made an appearance for the sake of the gossip mongers in town.

But within thirty minutes, the lasagna was in the oven, a workspace was set up at my dining room table, and Santiago and Sawyer were gathering sticks from the yard for a huge bonfire at the edge of the field. With the boys thoroughly entertained but our police presence still reliable, Mary and I each selected a book and began to read. Mary took the Morris volume she had already begun with, and I picked up Shifflett, to see if I could find anything new about Santiago's family, if this was the right Shifflett line.

Earnestine's work was modeled on the traditional genealogy books. She began with an introductory essay and then moved through the family tree, giving basic information about the people in each generation. It wasn't the most exciting reading, but it was thorough and well-done work. She had essentially documented the genealogies of almost every family at Bethel Baptist and some of the more prominent white families in Octonia, too. We had books for the Benfers and the Beazleys, as well as some other powerful Octonia folks like the Davenports and the Morrises.

Mary's first read was her own family's book, and the gasps and nods that were coming from her side of the table told me that Earnestine had done good work. I started with the Clevelands and read up through time until I reached Demetrius Cleveland the second, our Demetrius's great-great-grandfather. I saw where his family tree intersected with Mary's and with Earnestine's itself, and a bit of back and forth in the pages confirmed what I had suspected, most of the families at Bethel were kin to one another at least way back.

"You have a lot of cousins," I said to Mary.

She smiled. 'You aren't kidding. Holy cow. Do I have to send all these people birthday cards?"

"I think the rule is that you can stop once someone is twice removed, but you might want to confirm that." I smiled. I was glad we were able to keep this all light, on the surface at least. I could still feel the gnawing sense that we were about to stumble on something murder-worthy in our reading.

Forty-five minutes into our reading, the timer on the oven went off, and Mary stood to pull the pan of lasagna out while I poured out the bag of salad I tried to keep on standby. Then, I called in the boys, and we all sat down to eat.

It was always amazing to me how much more well-behaved Sawyer was when other people were around. He wasn't ever an unruly kid, but when guests were with us, he suddenly became a downright angel. Today, especially, that was nice since I didn't have much left in the tank to fight a battle over how many bites he'd eat. The boy ate two big pieces of lasagna and was then raring to get back to the fort he and Santiago were building in the backyard.

Part of me really wanted Santiago to stay with us, but more of me was glad that my son was having such a good time with a man who was more and more a crucial part of our lives. So I walked out with them to see their progress, which honestly looked like a ruin of a shack more than anything complete, and then went back in to study the Benfers' book.

Mary had already cleaned up, stored the leftovers in the fridge, and grabbed her own new read – the Morris book – by the time I came in. We settled side by side on the loveseat and dug in.

Every once in a while, one of us would lean forward to my laptop on the trunk in front of us, and do a quick search on a genealogy site. But mostly, we just skimmed page after page of family history.

I was just about into the twentieth century of the Benfers when I came across a listing for a woman named Ethel Lucy. She had married the man who was Nick and Levi's great-great-grandfather, Nick the Sixth. As I read Earnestine's notes about the Lucy family, I grabbed Mary's arm and began to read aloud:

THE LUCYS WERE *sharecroppers at the Benfer plantation, BelAirre. They had worked for the family for a least two generations, and so Nicholas asked for the young Ethel's hand in marriage, much of the community protested. Such crossing of class lines was not acceptable for many of our community's elite members.*

AND YET, *it was the story that broke soon after their wedding that really drew stares. Young Ethel was pregnant, a fact that her family tried to keep hidden but could not. Still, the baby was given away, at least that is what everyone was told, and soon, Ethel's public appearances became fewer and fewer.*

EARNESTINE'S NOTE ENDED THERE, but I had enough questions now that I didn't need more information. Mary's mouth was hanging open, "There are so many secrets in these pages that I can't keep straight who knew or who knows what." She held up the book that had been sitting on her lap. "But I do think Earnestine knew most everything."

I was just about to say I agreed and that it seemed like what she knew had gotten her killed when my phone rang. "Hi Mika," I said.

"Paisley, I need you to come to the store. Now." Her voice was shrill. "Alone. Don't even bring Sawyer."

I sucked in my breath. "I will be there in ten. Sit tight." I didn't know exactly what was going on, but Mika and I had been through enough together that we'd decided we needed a code to communicate when we were in distress. If either of us mentioned that Sawyer should not come, we knew it was serious. My friend was in big trouble.

My fear must have shone because Mary said, "What is it?"

"Mika's in trouble. I need to go. Alone. But I need you to tell Santiago that I will need him, secretly. And can you—?"

"I've got Sawyer. Be safe." She squeezed my hand and then jogged to the front door to tell our sheriff that we had a situation while I shouted a hurried goodbye to my son and hoped he could handle my quick departure. There was no time to waste.

14

I felt really bad about leaving Sawyer like I did, but if I was right, Mika was in real trouble and leaving Sawyer could take a half-hour if he was having a hard time. Better to just go and then reassure him later, especially if it meant keeping his Auntie Miks safe.

Besides, I knew Mary and Santiago would take good care of him, and I knew Santiago could be on his way behind me as soon as possible. Still, it felt like my stomach was in my mouth as I drove into town.

I tried to survey the scene as I pulled up about a block from Mika's store. I had thought about parking right up front in case she and I needed to make a run for it but had decided maybe me arriving with a tiny bit of surprise might give me some advantage. So I headed around the back of the store and let myself in quietly through the back door using Mika's security code.

Then, I stood quietly in the hallway and tried to listen. I couldn't make out any distinct words, and all the voices sounded like women. I took a small measure of comfort in that because at least it wasn't Levi Benfer, who was far bigger and stronger than I was. Most women I could take, I figured, if only because I sometimes carried around forty pounds of boy.

But when I peeked my head around the corner, all hopes of tackling anyone disappeared. Veronica Benfer was holding both Mika and Mrs. Stephenson at gunpoint.

Given what I'd read in Earnestine's Benfer book, I wasn't that surprised, but the fact that she'd come into a public place with a gun did unsettle me. No one who felt they had anything to lose did that kind of thing.

Veronica hadn't noticed me yet, but I saw Mika's eye widen as she caught sight of me. She shook her head and pretended to move her hair out of her eyes with the motion, and then she cut her eyes toward the back door. Her motion was quick, but Veronica still saw it. I had just enough time to dart back behind the wall before she turned in my direction.

Then, I hoped I had understood Mika's signal correctly and went back out the door I had come in. Just as I started to round the building to reenter through the main door to the shop, I ran into Santiago. He'd added a baseball cap to the jeans and T-shirt he'd changed into at my house earlier, and if I didn't know his form so well, I might not have immediately recognized him.

He pulled me toward him and held me tight as he whispered in my ear. "What's going on?"

Anyone walking by would just think we an amorous couple in an embrace, which made me a little uneasy since that action indicated that Santiago was very concerned about appearances. I put my arms around his back and whispered, "Veronica Benfer. Gun on Mika and Mrs. Stephenson."

I felt Santiago stiffen, as my words registered. "What's Mika's back door code?" He asked as he pulled me even tighter to him.

I whispered the six digits into his ear and then gave him a quick kiss that I hoped looked like I was saying goodbye. Then, we parted, and I walked right up to the front door of Mika's shop and strolled in. I hoped my acting skills were up to par as I faked surprised at seeing Veronica there, and given that she simply said, "Hello" and used the gun to point me toward Mika and Mrs. Stephenson, I didn't think she was suspicious.

I walked slowly toward the counter as I hoped I was giving Santiago enough time to make his entrance and maybe even call Savannah for back-up. "What is going on here? Veronica what are you doing?" I tried to sound concerned and not let on just how angry and afraid I was.

Veronica sighed. "I expect you already know, don't you?"

"Know what?" I said.

"I know that you found Mrs. Greene's hidey-hole, and I know you well enough, Paisley. You couldn't wait to read what was in there, could you?" Her voice was icy but also a bit heavy with what I thought were tears. "I figured she had her information stashed somewhere near her house, but I was hoping it had gone down in the demolition." She pulled her fingers through her hair roughly.

My brain raced as I tried to think of how much of the truth would serve us here. "The shack behind the church that is full of old books. Is that what you mean?"

Veronica rolled her eyes. "So you did read them?"

I groaned. I had shown my hand when I tried to play too dumb about exactly what we'd found. Veronica knew my historian's heart would have dived right into those pages. I scrambled for a good answer. "I did read a couple, the Clevelands and Morrises, since were looking for information about them. But they didn't tell us anything we didn't already know." I was telling the truth, of course, but only part of it. I hoped she couldn't tell that.

She studied my face. "So you were just doing what I hired you to do?" Her voice sounded hopeful.

"Exactly. When I saw those books, I thought they might give us more information, so this afternoon, I read them cover to cover and made notes." I smiled, hoping that somehow I was convincing her of the truth in what I was saying.

She nodded. "Did you find anything new for Hortense or Levi?"

I shook my head and tried to keep from smiling since those kind of questions made me think I was leading her down the right path. If she didn't know I'd read anything about her family, maybe she'd just leave. Even in the moment I realized I was being naïve. After all, a woman who has just held people at gunpoint is probably on a path of no return. But I had to try. "Not a thing," I said. "I think the books are just about members at Bethel."

The gun lowered a bit as Veronica appeared to mull over that idea. But then, I saw her jaw tighten, and she raised the gun until it was level with my face. "I don't know if you actually believe that to be true, Paisley, or just want me to believe it. Either way, it doesn't really matter because they aren't just about folks there. If they were, Nick's grandfather wouldn't have felt it necessary to kill that pastor's wife."

On the other side of Mika, Mrs. Stephenson gasped, and Mika grabbed my hand. "So it was Nick's grandfather who pushed her down the stairs?" I said.

Veronica let out a long sigh. "Yes. He couldn't let her find out the truth, but she couldn't help herself. She just kept digging, kept asking questions. When she asked about the Lucys, his grandfather knew she had gotten too close." She leaned back against a shelf full of yarn.

"I don't mean to be rude, Veronica, "Mika said, "but what secret was it so important to keep?"

"Nick's grandfather loved his grandmother, Ethel Lucy. He really did. He didn't want her shamed, and he didn't want their baby to be humiliated. They married, and he thought he'd stopped the rumors," Veronica said as she stared off into the distance above our heads.

"But he hadn't, had he?" I said quietly. "Everyone already knew."

She nodded. "They knew. "She looked up at met my eyes. "But people don't know now do they? We are free of that shame. Nick and I can live without the taint of his grandfather —" She stopped speaking abruptly.

"Nick's father was of another time. Nick doesn't get it, but I do. All these secrets. The shame of his birth. His dad—"

"Was conceived outside of marriage," Mrs. Stephenson said quickly, and I appreciated the kindness of her words. "They loved each other, though. You said that? So why hide now?" Her voice was kind, understanding.

Veronica shook her head. "Just too many secrets, and the Benfers have done so much good for this town. I didn't want their name tainted."

At that moment, Savannah strolled in the front door and pretended to be looking at a bin at the front of the store. I resisted my urge to look at the back door to find Santiago and kept my gaze on Veronica, who was moving backward toward Savannah now, never taking her eyes off of us.

I was sure Savannah knew Veronica had a gun, but she kept browsing, moving slowly closer to the armed woman even as Veronica closed the gap between them, careful to keep the gun close to her body.

Savannah looked over Veronica's head to Mika and said, "Do you have any more of this alpaca in another color? I'm thinking of trying my first cardigan."

Her words were followed by a quick jerk of her arm on the stack of crates she was studying, and the entire stack of plastic and alpaca fiber fell right onto Veronica's head.

Without hesitation, Savannah grabbed the gun from Veronica's hand as the woman lay on the floor, and then Santiago stepped in with his own gun drawn on Veronica. "Don't move, Mrs. Benfer," he said.

Veronica's face crumpled, and she fell back on the floor and began to cry. As Savannah cuffed her and then got her a bottle of water from Mika's mini-fridge, Santiago checked on the three of us. "You okay?"

Each of us nodded, and then we spun toward each other and fell into hug and tears. We were safe, but we were still terrified.

ONCE VERONICA WAS FORMALLY ARRESTED and taken to the police station for booking, I called Mary and asked her to bring Sawyer over right away. I wanted to hug him and apologize for leaving so abruptly. Then, I called my dad and Lucille and asked if they could come with snacks and something alcoholic to help us settle.

Mrs. Stephenson called her husband, Ben, who came over right away as did Saul as soon as Mika texted him. Within an hour, all the people we loved best in the world were gathered in Mika's now-closed shop. Most of us had mint juleps that Lucille whipped up, and the plate of rugelach she'd brought over was almost empty. The mood was still quiet in the store, but I could feel a lightening of my stress as I thought about all the mysteries that we had solved today.

Lucille refreshed my drink and then took a seat next to me in the Cozy Corner. "You okay?" she asked. I looked over at Sawyer, who was busy making another giant spider web and teaching his grandfather how to do the same. He'd not even been upset when he arrived because Mary had said I'd gotten called away to be a superhero. He was frustrated that I had left my cape at home, but since he'd brought it for me, I figured even that was made right in his world.

"I am," I said. "Mostly. Just sad that something as insignificant as an interracial family and baby born out of marriage could cause this must pain."

"It's despicable, of course," Lucille said. "But those were different times. Shame was bigger somehow, at least about things like that." She looked over at Sawyer. "Still though . . ."

Just then, Santiago came in and headed right toward me, taking my hands and pulling me up into a tight hug before urging me to sit back down and have more to drink. "I'm so glad you are okay. You are one brave woman," he said as he squeezed onto the arm of my chair next to me.

I blushed. "I didn't think about being brave. I just thought Mika was in trouble." It was the truth. I realized now that I had been foolhardy, but I hadn't considered anything but helping my friend in the moment. I sighed. "Did Veronica tell you anything else?"

Santiago sat back and took the julep Lucille handed him. "She unraveled when we got her into the interrogation room. Savannah is still with her. We're a bit worried about her mental state."

I sighed. "Yeah, she didn't seem quite lucid or all together."

"She's not. She kept rambling about how if she'd only known the hidey-hole was right there, then everything would have been alright, whatever that means." Santiago shrugged.

"It means she knew that Earnestine had records that might reveal the Benfer family secret but hadn't been able to find them," I said. "She saw herself as the protector of the family. It was an honorable motive, at least. Maybe." I shrugged.

The bell over the front door rang, and Levi and Nick came in. Seeing them together lit a realization in my mind. "You two aren't twins," I said as they approached.

Nick sighed. "No, we aren't. Two years apart." He knelt down. "I'm so sorry, Paisley. I didn't want to put you in danger, and I didn't think I was. But Veronica was so adamant that we find out what we could that I didn't want to say no."

Santiago sat forward. "You knew she was in a mentally fragile place?"

Levi nodded. "We all did. But when she found out that Paisley had searched the entire parish house and didn't mention anything about our family's secrets, her mood lifted. It seemed like she was really looking forward to your research, like maybe she'd be able to pour herself into other family stories and let this one go."

I sighed. "I'm so sorry. I had no idea that my research was going to hurt her so much."

Lucille grabbed my hands. "You did nothing wrong, Paisley. You found the truth." She looked up at Nick and Levi. "The irony, of course, is that no one in your family did anything wrong until your grandfather murdered Earnestine."

"And then here we are today," Nick said with a frown. "We need to get to Veronica. But we wanted to come apologize first." They turned, spoke to Mika and then Mrs. Stephenson, and then left.

"What was that all about?" Mary asked as she came over and sat down with us.

"A bit of the sins of the father being visited upon the sons and daughter," I said. Suddenly, I was very, very sad.

FORTUNATELY, Mika had the perfect way to keep me from sinking too deeply into sorrow – our first day at the Charlottesville City Market was the following morning, and given the events of the week, we had done absolutely nothing to prepare.

So Mrs. Stephenson whipped us all into action and soon had us packing yarn into totes, making signage, and putting together cross-stitch kits with the patterns my dad had burned into thin planks of wood so that children could learn to stitch a holiday ornament on something easier than floppy fabric.

As we were finishing up, Demetrius and Hortense came in after having received a call from Nick Benfer about the events of the day. They offered their sincere apologies for their cousin's behavior and said that they were all working together to get Veronica the help she needed after she had her day in court.

Then, we all loaded up my car and Mika's car for the farmer's market the next day while Demetrius called the Pierce Inn to see if they had a room we could use for a burger bar in a half-hour.

That is one of the perks of a small town – even the best restaurant usually has space for you at the last minute. So we all walked over and enjoyed great burgers while we tried to forget just how messed up our world could be, at least for a few minutes.

THEN NEXT MORNING, I dropped Sawyer off early at his dad's, and he was delighted to see that the slip and slide was already out and ready for him. He gave me a behind-the-back wave goodbye, and I headed into town to meet Mika at her shop.

I was very surprised to see Dad, Lucille, and Mary there when I arrived, but when they said they were coming to help us at the market, I almost cried. I had been worried that we couldn't handle the kind of traffic that came through, and I was so very tired from the events of the week.

When we pulled up to our spot, a prime location at a corner near the walking mall in the city, Santiago was already there with two canopies open and three tables lined up at the front of our space. He was in the process of putting out camping chairs, and when I saw him, I ran to him, kissed him deeply, and said a heartfelt thank you. Now, I was excited about the day.

Soon, we had our "Stitches and Yarns" sign up on the front of the table, and Lucille had set up her phone with the new mobile credit card machine Mika had ordered. All of our merchandise was displayed on the tables, and Mika had brought a few of her handmade items to hang around the tent for sale and to add visual interest.

While the four of us women finished with the details of our booth, Dad and Santiago went to get us savory crepes from the booth down the way, and soon, the customers started rolling in. Dad's picture frames went fast as did the one coffee table he'd made as a sample for custom orders. My cross-stitch kits were a big hit, and Mika sold out of all the hand-spun yarn she had brought with her as well as several baby sweaters she'd had on display.

The day went by briskly, especially since the guys kept us plied with good food and drinks from our fellow business owners. And by the end of the day, we had more than doubled the money we had put into the booth, given out dozens of business cards, and had a ton of fun in the process. Before we left, Mika booked us for the next three weekends, and I found I was looking forward to it.

Just as the market closed in the early afternoon, Demetrius Cleveland stopped by and asked if we all had time for a little pit stop on the way back to Octonia. I was exhausted and really ready to cross-stitch and watch TV, but he seemed so excited that I didn't have it in me to say no.

He led our caravan of vehicles through downtown Charlottesville and over to the grounds of the University of Virginia. After we parked in the garage and walked up to the main level of the campus, we saw there, right in front of the Rotunda, a group of people gathered around a central circle. Many of them were dressed in colorful regalia that was covered in beads and feathers, and under one tent at the edge of the circle, three men and a woman were beating a drum and singing.

As we approached, Chief Stephenson stepped out to meet us. She was dressed in a long deerskin skirt and a matching top with delicate fringe decorated with white beads at the base of both pieces. In her silvering hair, she had two feathers attached to a beautiful, beaded headband. "Welcome to our celebration," she said as she hugged each of us.

"Thank you," I said. "What are we celebrating?"

"All of us," she said as she took my hand and led me to the circle. "Our ancestors and our stories. The truth coming to light. New friends." She left us standing at the edge of the circle as she and a group of women took to the center and began to dance.

Order Paisley's Next Adventure, *Stitch X For Murder*, here - https://books2read.com/stitchxformurder

GREAT READS AND A FREE NOVELLA

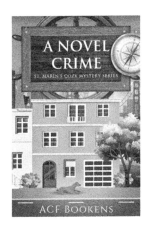

Join my Cozy Up email group for weekly book recs & a FREE copy of *A Novel Crime*, the prequel to my St. Marin's Cozy Mystery Series.
Sign-up here - https://bookens.andilit.com/CozyUp

ALSO BY ACF BOOKENS

St. Marin's Cozy Mystery Series

Publishable By Death

Entitled To Kill

Bound To Execute

Plotted For Murder

Tome To Tomb

Scripted To Slay

Proof Of Death

Epilogue of An Epitaph - Coming October 2021

Hardcover Homicide - Coming December 2021

Stitches In Crime Series

Crossed By Death

Bobbins and Bodies

Hanged By A Thread

Counted Corpse

Stitch X For Murder - Coming in November 2021

Sewn At The Crime - Coming in January 2022

ABOUT THE AUTHOR

ACF Bookens lives in the Southwest Mountains of Virginia, where the mountain tops remind her that life is a rugged beauty of a beast worthy of our attention. When she's not writing, she enjoys chasing her son around the house with the full awareness she will never catch him, cross-stitching while she binge-watches police procedurals, and reading everything she can get her hands on. Find her at bookens.andilit.com.

 facebook.com/bookenscozymysteries

Made in the USA
Monee, IL
28 December 2021

87441133R00108